The Night Heroes:

Moth Man

The Night Heroes:

Moth Man

Dr. Bo Wagner

Word of His Mouth Publishers
Mooresboro, NC

ISBN: 978-1-941039-96-0
Printed in the United States of America
© 2017 Dr. Bo Wagner (Robert Arthur Wagner)

Word of His Mouth Publishers
Mooresboro, NC
www.wordofhismouth.com

Cover art by Chip Nuhrah and Dana Wagner

Moth Man

My breath was coming in gasps, and I could feel the tears stinging my eyes as I ran, panicked, through the pitch-black West Virginia night. There was no use telling me that there is no such thing as the Moth Man. Yesterday, I would have agreed with you, but now I could not shake him, nor could I find Kyle or Aly, and I knew I was going to die...

Chapter One

There are mountains, and then there are MOUNTAINS. By this I mean, there really is no other place quite like West Virginia. I have often described it as a state that used to be flat and about the size of Texas that God put a hand on each side of and squeezed it inward until all the beauty went straight up.

Anyway, I was for about the thirtieth time in my short life riding through those lovely mountains and valleys of West Virginia. By short life, I mean that I am currently fifteen years old. So, why in the world would a fifteen-year-old boy from North Carolina be going to West Virginia that many times, you ask? That's easy; I am a PK, a preacher's kid, specifically an evangelist's kid. My dad preaches meetings all over the United States and even in many different countries, and when he does, my mom and my two sisters and I go with him.

My mom was, at the current moment, sitting in the front seat beside my dad, navigating. Dad, bless his heart, is as strong as a bull and is a certified genius, but he is also directionally challenged. This is to say that if mom was not along for the ride, we would all soon be hopelessly lost, GPS or not.

I looked to my left in the middle row of our trusty Yukon and saw the older of my two sisters, raven-haired Carrie, with her fourteen-year-old nose predictably stuck in a book. She generally missed most of the beauty of the surroundings that we drove through because of her penchant for reading. I didn't mind, though. She is the other genius in the family, and that brain of hers has come in handy, no, scratch that, it has literally been a lifesaver on more than one occasion for us.

In the third row behind the two of us was the youngest and smallest of us all, my twelve-year-old sister Aly. She is the lightning in a bottle of our team; volatile, unpredictable, but utterly loyal, and unstoppable when she sets her mind to something.

Our team, by the way, is the Night Heroes.

It was in this very same state, West Virginia, that the Night Heroes came into being. My dad was preaching a meeting in Boomer. While sleeping in a Sunday school room in the middle of the night, Carrie and Aly and I were awakened in the night by the voice of a train conductor. He called us each by name, and when we all sat up to find out what was going on, we found ourselves one hundred years or so in the past! If you have read our previous books, you know by now that we were sent on a mission to rescue a little boy who was being held prisoner by some very bad men in a coal mine. Since that time, we have gone on to rescue a girl from a concentration camp in World War II, we have kept two brothers from killing each other during the Battle of Chickamauga, we have gotten embroiled in an Indian war, we have dealt with a pirate off the coast of North Carolina, and we have unraveled a Mayan mystery.

Through all of these adventures, we have learned a little bit more each time of what we can do. We learned early on that when we wake up in the past we have exactly five days to get each mission done. At the end of each day in the past, as long as we are not being held prisoner, we can go to sleep somewhere and wake up back in our own time just as refreshed as if we had gotten a full night's sleep. But if we have gotten any injuries in the past, we carry those injuries with us into our time.

We also learned that whatever we go to sleep with each night we can carry with us from the present to the past or vice versa. That is incredibly helpful; it has allowed us to bring a few necessary tools into the past with us from time to time to get the job done.

Our conductor ushers us to the mission each day and then leaves us to our task.

Some weeks we go to a meeting with my dad, and everything is very normal and uneventful. We never know when the call in the night is going to come.

It had been a few weeks since our last adventure, which we called *When Serpents Rise*. We had been to meetings in our home state of North Carolina, then Tennessee, Ohio, and Alabama. But like I said, we were now heading to the mountains of West Virginia and would not be stopping until we got to the Ohio state line. Dad would be preaching a meeting at the Jordan Baptist Church in Gallipolis Ferry, West Virginia. It would be held in conjunction with Grace Baptist Church right nearby in Point Pleasant, West Virginia. Both are hard up against the Ohio state line, and we would actually be staying in Gallipolis, Ohio.

"Are we theeeeeeerrrrre yet?"

That, of course, would be Aly. She asks that question roughly four times a minute from the time we get in the vehicle at the beginning of the trip until the time we get out of it.

"Sure thing, honey bunny, tuck and roll."

If you have read our books, you have heard that before. That would be our dad, who was presently urging the Yukon forward at about sixty miles per hour.

Aly just groaned and banged the back of her impatient head against the headrest. Carrie looked up momentarily from her book and in a very professorial tone said, "Scientists are presently very diligently working on a methodology to bend time and space to allow us to get across great distances in an instantaneous moment. Until then, perhaps we should do something very valuable and scholarly..."

I groaned because I knew what was coming. Sure enough...

"A in that license tag."

"B right there on that Bosley Hair Replacement for Men sign."

The alphabet game. Doesn't it always go the exact same way? The letters roll like crazy until X, then it all bogs down for what seems like an eternity.

"X in Exit 7 for Pomeroy/Gallipolis!" Carrie shouted. From there it was Y for yield, Z on a license tag right ahead of us (Carrie, for the win), and then a big beautiful S on the Super Eight sign that told us our aching legs were about to get a good stretch.

Chapter Two

We all piled out of the Yukon with groans and stretches and pops. Dad, ever the impatient one, was immediately giving orders as to who should carry what. It really wasn't necessary; we had all done this so many times that we knew exactly what to do. Still, it is in dad's genetic makeup to tell us anyway, so none of us minded.

It took us about ten minutes to get checked in to room 107 and begin setting up shop for the week. Mom, the absolute heartbeat of our family, was immediately ironing clothes while simultaneously helping my sisters get ready for the night service and telling dad and me which bags had everything located in them that we needed. Honestly, sometimes I think she has four brains in her head all capable of processing different thoughts and tasks at the exact same time.

"Okay, Warner brats," (that would be dad's affectionate name for us) "you have two churches and two pastors to be remembering and serving this week. Kyle, what are the two churches?"

"Jordan Baptist and Grace Baptist, sir," I said with a military cadence.

"Carrie, who is the pastor of Jordan Baptist?"

Carrie loved this kind of thing, so she snapped to attention and saluted as she said, "Sir, yes, sir! The pastor of Jordan Baptist is Bo Burgess, sir."

"Well done, Lance Corporal Carrie. Aly, who is the pastor of Grace Baptist?"

"Like, John Pinson!"

She said that with a wicked grin, and I knew she was playfully trying to get under dad's skin. I also knew since he could not stand the word "like" being used in that manner that it would work, maybe better than she intended.

"Like? Like, in some instances is a verb, as in 'I like proper grammar, especially when my children use it.' Like, in other instances, can even be a preposition, as in 'mischievous daughters are a lot like cattle; they often end up with their hides tanned."

Aly harumphed. Carrie nodded her head in intellectual admiration and agreement. Me? I was rolling on the floor laughing. Nice shot, dad, nice shot. I knew he did not mean it

14

for a second, our spanking days ended years ago, but it was still hilarious nonetheless.

Our ever-patient mom just kept plugging right along, getting everyone and everything ready. I never cease to be amazed at the transformation she can make in three teenagers and one ultra type A personality adult male. We had pulled into the hotel at 6 o'clock sharp looking wrinkled and worn, and everyone's hair looked like an explosion in a mattress factory. We pulled back out of the hotel at 6:30 with nary a wrinkle and not a single hair out of place. This is something both of my parents have taught all of us children for a very long time; going to God's house to worship the Lord is one of the most important things we can ever do and, as such, deserves the very best out of all of us, including our appearance.

We had been to the Grace Baptist Church in Point Pleasant before, but this would be our first time at the Jordan Baptist Church in Gallipolis Ferry. It took us about ten minutes to get from the hotel to Clendenin Pike Road. And then about a half a mile later we saw a lovely little white church up on the left, and we knew we had arrived.

Going to a new church is always a lot of fun. We meet new people and quickly make new friends. This meeting would be sort of a double blessing since we would be getting to meet new people and make new friends and also get to see some old friends from Grace Baptist.

Pastor Burgess was the first one to arrive and greet us. He is about my dad's height and thick with muscle. I think he would be a good person not to mess with. Right behind him was his wife Ashley, a super-nice lady, and right behind her were their three cute kids, Thanael, Sloan, and Lann. In very short order other vehicles started pouring into the parking lot, and soon Pastor John Pinson was standing in our little circle alongside Pastor Burgess and my dad. Pastor Pinson was a police officer for many years, but just a few years ago went into the ministry full-time. That is sort of a hero to hero proposition; he has gone from saving lives to saving souls.

Within just a few minutes Pastor Burgess made his way to the pulpit and all of the folks standing around talking made their way into the pews. We sat in the back, as we always do. Dad says that he always has to be in front of people night after night, so he likes being behind people and being as unnoticed as possible until he gets called up. As to our order on the pew, there was exactly one rule that was never violated: dad gets the end.

I don't know if other families are like this, but for our family, it is the other spots that cause a lot of wrangling. I am just over six feet tall now with long legs, so I would love to have the end so I can stretch one leg out a little bit, but I know dad will never give that spot up. That means that normally I try to get the other end of the pew. Whether or not I do so usually depends upon the length of the pew itself. If the pew is too long for mom to be able to grab my ear if necessary, normally I do not get the spot on the other end. In this case, she felt comfortably within grabbing distance, so that left the other three spots up for grabs.

Both of the girls wanted to sit beside dad. They always get all Bambi-eyed and claim that it is because they love him so much, but I suspect that both of them simply want to be on the end when he finally gets up to preach.

Anyway, on this night the order ended up as dad, Carrie, mom, Aly, and then me on the other end. And after some announcements and a few wonderful special songs and a congregational or two, dad was heading for the pulpit to preach.

On this night he preached one of his favorite messages; a message that a lot of people across the country have gotten help from, "Maybe Your Storm Isn't for You." I have heard it so many times, and it still strikes me as amazing to realize that a demon-possessed man got delivered by Jesus because he saw others going through a storm and saw Jesus working on their behalf.

Once again, the invitation saw people flooding the altars and crying out to God as they laid their hearts bare before Him. I knew that was exactly what my dad wanted. He often says, "I can't be there for you at all times, and neither can your pastor. But Jesus can, so why don't you come and talk to Him..."

I am so glad that I know the Jesus that my dad preaches about. I wish everybody in the world did; I can't imagine how people live without Him.

A few minutes later Pastor Burgess was concluding the service, and folks were either milling about fellowshipping with each other or heading for their cars to go home. We, along with Pastor Burgess and Pastor Pinson, were about to engage in one of my favorite activities: an after-church supper. Bob Evans this time, home of some of the best desserts your mouth will ever usher into your stomach.

It took us about ten minutes to get back there; it just so happens to be across the parking lot from our hotel. That would make it convenient for us to waddle back to our rooms after we had stuffed ourselves.

We ate and talked and laughed and had a great time for about an hour, then we said our goodbyes and walked over to the hotel while our hosts drove themselves home. I was looking up as we walked, marveling at the beautiful sky overhead. The streetlights and the glow of the businesses could not completely dim the glory of God's tapestry. Beside me, I could hear Carrie whispering softly, "The heavens declare the glory of God; and the firmament sheweth his handywork." I looked over at her, and my brainiac sister was looking up and marveling at the same sky that I was. We may fight and fuss and argue like normal brothers and sisters, but I sure do love that girl, and Aly too.

But the walk was short, too short really, and we were once again in room 107 preparing for a good night's sleep. We prayed together as a family just as we do every single night. We have done that every night since we were babies, and I know that mom and dad had done it even before we came along. I tell you, there is nothing better than being raised in a Christian family.

But sleep is pretty good too, and it didn't take long for five Warners to be softly snoring in rhythm to the hum of the air conditioner, which was, of course, set to somewhere around "make a penguin put on a coat."

Chapter Three

My heart was pounding out of my chest. I was sitting straight up on my air mattress on the floor, and a cold sweat was dripping down my face. Instinctively I looked over toward my sisters, willing my eyes to adjust to the darkness. They were still sound asleep; mom and dad were too.

I shook my head back and forth, trying to get the cobwebs out. What had awakened me so abruptly, why was I so scared? I have jumped out of an airplane and fought a knife-wielding Indian; I should not get this rattled over a dream.

It was the eyes. Those red, glowing, hate-filled eyes.

I closed my own very brown eyes and took a few very deep, slow breaths. I needed to get my emotions under control.

At that moment I heard Carrie and Aly begin to rustle in their bed, and even whimper a little bit. I watched for a few seconds, and they began to get more and more agitated. I don't know how I knew, but somehow, I just knew I needed to wake them up.

"Hey, guys," I hissed, and I reached over to shake their bed just a little bit. Oh man, when I did, what a reaction! They both sat straight up in bed with their eyes absolutely huge, and I knew they were both about to scream, and I had a good idea why. As quick as a flash, I put a hand over both of their mouths.

"Shoooosh! It's me, Kyle; it's okay," I whispered.

At once, all three of us looked over to mom and dad, and thankfully they were both still sound asleep. I grabbed both of the girls and pulled them out of bed and down onto the floor with me. They were both shaking like leaves, and Aly grabbed me in a bear hug and sobbed quietly. There was no way she was going to be able to talk for a while, so I looked over at Carrie, she looked right back at me, and both of us murmured two words: "Red eyes."

Carrie joined the hug, and we all just sat there for a moment drawing comfort and reassurance from one another's presence. Finally, we invited a fourth person into the embrace.

"Lord," I began to pray softly, "I don't know exactly what is going on right now. We three have been through so much together, and each new adventure seems to build greater confidence in us. Maybe in a way that has actually become a negative, Lord. Perhaps we have begun to rely on our own strength and understanding. And yet, Lord, You told us in Proverbs 3:5-6 'Trust in the LORD with all thine heart; and lean not unto thine own understanding. In all thy ways acknowledge him, and he shall direct thy paths.'

"Lord, this is not starting like anything we have ever been through thus far. We need You to guide us and to tell us what You need us to do. We need You to give us Your strength and Your courage. These things we pray in Jesus name, Amen."

Aly's sobbing subsided, and I could feel all of our heartbeats slowing to where they needed to be. We held each other for a couple more minutes, and then Carrie, who had been the quietest of all, spoke.

"Guys, I know this doesn't make much sense, but we need to go outside."

Aly tensed up immediately and squeezed me as if her life depended on it. She was shaking her head "no." I held her without taking my eyes off of Carrie, but I had learned enough to know that she doesn't say things rashly or without reason.

"What do you mean, Sis?"

"While we were praying, while you were asking God to guide us and help us to follow Him, I believe the Lord spoke to my heart. I am pretty sure He wants us to very quietly go outside."

I let out a long and low breath at that.

"Sis, are you sure? That sounds a whole lot like sneaking out in the middle of the night, which is something no kids ought to ever, ever do."

"I know, Kyle, I know. And if this were a matter of sin, if I were suggesting that we go out cruising around or getting into trouble or looking for fun then even I would disagree with me. But we all woke up having the exact same dream. We are used to being called away in the middle of the night by our Conductor, who we know is sent by God Himself. I am absolutely sure God laid this on my heart. It won't take but a minute, and if I'm wrong, we can come right back in."

I looked down at Aly, and she looked up at me. I was expecting to see fear on her face, but her look was changing to become far more "Aly-like." By that I mean, I was actually starting to see a bit of anger and a bit of spunk creep back onto her face.

"I am okay with this, Kyle. Someone or something ruined my night, and whatever it is I intend on gnawing its leg off up to the kneecap."

I grinned at my pint-sized, stick-of-dynamite of a sister, and said, "Okay then. We go very quietly, we take a room card with us, and if we don't have a very good reason to stay outside after thirty seconds, we come right back in, forget all of this, and go back to bed."

The girls nodded at me, and we started sliding our shoes and socks on, and all of us instinctively reached for the small night packs that we always carry with us to bed each night in case of an adventure.

Two minutes later, creeping like cat burglars, we slid out of the room and down the hallway.

It was eerie; there was no one around even at the desk out front. Everything seemed far dimmer than it should have. We were all as tense as violin strings as we made our way out the front door and into the parking lot. Every step we took made things feel weirder and weirder, but we knew where we needed to go. For there, standing with his back to us, was the Conductor.

"Good evening, Sir," I said as we slipped up beside him. "This is an odd way to start a mission. This is the first time you haven't called us into the past; in fact, it is the first time that you didn't actually call us."

He did not look at us; he just continued to stare straight ahead in the direction of Point Pleasant.

"You are correct on the second point, but you may want to check up on that first point."

Suddenly, I got a very weird feeling in my gut. I knew that the "first point" was about him not calling us into the past. Slowly, very slowly, my sisters and I turned around to face our hotel.

It was gone.

And so was the Silver Memorial Bridge which, just a few hours earlier, had been standing right beside it crossing the Ohio River.

Chapter Four

I have not had a sinking feeling in my stomach quite like that since the first time I jumped out of an airplane. So much looked the same, but so much locked very different as well.

"Well, Carrie," the conductor said with a wry smile, "you know how we usually begin, so what do you think?"

"Where and when, I know," Carrie said matter-of-factly. "As to the where, that is very easy to figure out. We are still in Gallipolis, Ohio, just a few miles from Point Pleasant, West Virginia. We are, in fact, standing right where the parking lot of the hotel of the Super Eight was just a few hours ago. Now, here is where things get weird. In every other mission on which we have been sent, we have been a hundred years or more into the past. Most commonly we are actually one hundred fifty or two hundred years or more into the past. In this case, the year is 1966."

I jolted just a little bit at that. That was a very, very specific year, which told me Carrie was not guessing, at all.

"How do you know that it is exactly 1966, Sis?"

"Well, let's start with the obvious. As of very late 1967 on this spot, construction began on the Silver Memorial Bridge, and it was completed in 1969. That bridge was the replacement for the Silver Bridge which collapsed in December 1967. That bridge was a mile upstream of this one. It stood from 1928 until 1967. If you look off in the distance, you will see the lights on it; it is still standing."

Aly and I both followed Carrie's finger with our eyes, and sure enough, we saw the lights on the bridge in the distance. So, we knew that it was definitely pre-December of 1967.

"Okay, so before 1967," Aly said. "But how do you peg it at exactly 1966?"

"Check out the car billboard behind you."

Both Aly and I whirled around to see, and an ear-to-ear grin immediately crossed my face.

"Sis, if dad knew about this, you would go up an extra four notches in his already high estimation of you."

The billboard was of an old Camaro. Old to our day, that is, but clearly brand-new on the sign and in the lot. Old Camaros are my dad's absolute favorite car. He likes the 1969 best, but they first came out in 1966. So, since the bridge told us that it was before 1967, that left only one year. As usual, my genius sister had missed nothing and had taken a bunch of random clues and arrived at a perfect bull's-eye. I looked over at the Conductor, and he was smiling in satisfaction.

"Very nice work, as always, Young Lady."

"Thank you, Sir," she replied politely. "And now may I ask you a question?"

He breathed in deeply, let it out in a sigh, and replied, "You may, but by now you should know that, depending on the question, I may or may not be allowed to answer."

"I understand. Here is the question: does our mission here somehow involve the dream of evil red eyes that awakened all three of us?"

"It does," he said very seriously. "But at this point, that is all that I can say about that other than to tell you that there is more than one form of warfare."

That sounded pretty ominous to me. But I had a question of my own that I wanted answered.

"Sir, here is another question for you. In every other mission, we have gone far enough back into the past that there was no risk of anyone in the present knowing us. But with this being 1966, there is actually a reasonably good chance that some little boy or little girl that we run into during our mission could be an old man or an old woman sitting in the pews of the church where my dad is preaching revival this week. What exactly are we supposed to do about that?"

The conductor put his hands on my shoulders and said, "I would suggest that you be careful." Then he laughed a deep belly laugh, and suddenly I felt like I was talking to my dad since that is the exact kind of answer he tends to give us.

During the few seconds of the conductor laughing and me shaking my head, Aly stepped right beside us with her arms crossed. That is normally the posture she takes when she has a "frustruestion," which is my name for one of her "frustrated questions."

"Okay, my turn. What exactly are we doing here? Should we just wander around the streets randomly waiting to get mugged? And how are we to get around; are we on the ankle express?"

Aly was not normally that curt, and I knew that her current attitude was rooted in the deep heartfelt fear we had all been awakened to. The Conductor seemed to know that as he answered, because his voice was as kind and soothing as a loving grandfather, with no hint of scolding over her attitude.

"As to your mission, head into Point Pleasant and you will quickly figure it out. And, though all three of you have proven very adept at running very fast and very far, in this case, I have procured other transportation for you."

As he said that, he pointed toward the street lamp, and I noticed three bicycles parked beside it. Well, this would be a first for us. We have jumped out of planes, sailed on ships, paddled in canoes, ridden trains, been in wagons, and done a lot of running, but we have not been pedal pushers on a mission before.

"Are you guys up for this?" I asked Carrie and Aly. Somehow, I knew the reaction that I would get.

"Are you up for it?"

"Yes, littlest sister, I do believe I am. But I suggest before we hop and pedal that we kneel and pray."

And so once again we began this mission like every other, bowing three limited, still-a-lot-to-learn minds and hearts before the all-knowing God, and asking for His guidance.

Somehow, we knew we would need it more than ever.

As is so often the case, before our prayer was done and our eyes opened, our Conductor was gone. And somehow the lack of his presence quickly allowed the cloud of fear from moments earlier to start settling on our hearts again.

"Let's remember what the Lord said," Carrie reminded, " 'I will never leave thee nor forsake thee.' We don't know exactly what we are facing, but we know the God who does know what we are facing."

Aly and I nodded solemnly, and we all mounted our metallic steeds.

Chapter Five

Kids today have it so easy. Yeah, yeah, I know I am actually a kid, and I am actually in today when I am not in some far distant yesterday. But for the moment I had a very good point of reference for my complaint. We children of the 21st century, used to very comfortable ten and fifteen-speed bikes, were at the moment bouncing along on ancient metallic dinosaurs. I felt every bump and pothole in the road as we whizzed (more like clattered and rattled, actually) along the streets heading into Point Pleasant.

We pulled into the Tiny's Drive-In and wheeled to a stop. Our breathing was all still very measured and easy; we were used to some pretty extreme exertion.

As we took in the surroundings, it felt a lot like being in an old black-and-white television show. The buildings were mostly made of gray block. There were streetlights, but nowhere near as many as we would have in our day and nowhere near as bright.

The drive-in was closed. I knew that if we were in this exact same spot tomorrow night after church, whatever business occupied it would likely still be open.

As our eyes absorbed the setting, our ears begin to play their part as well. From just a few blocks away the sound of the bells from the Christ Episcopal Church begin to peal.

And with each time that it did, more and more color drained out of the faces of three kids on bikes in a parking lot who were expecting the sun to come up at any moment.

Eight... nine... ten... eleven... twelve...

The three of us just looked at each other, and it was Aly who finally said what all of us were thinking. "Well guys, I don't think we are going to be seeing any sunlight on this particular mission."

"How? How in the world can it be midnight?"

"Well, Kyle," Carrie answered heavily, " 'a.m.' and 'p.m.' stand for 'ante meridiem' and 'post meridiem,' which mean 'before noon' and 'after noon,' respectively. Since noon is neither before noon nor after noon, a designation of either a.m. or p.m. is incorrect. Having therefore established what, and when, noon is, we can arrive at a designation for midnight, since midnight is both twelve hours before noon and twelve hours after noon."

"Thank you for that completely intellectual yet thoroughly unhelpful sarcasm, Sis. I think you know what I mean by my question. In every single mission we have ever been on, we have operated during daylight hours. Not one thing about this mission is starting off in any semblance of a normal fashion."

"No, it really isn't," Carrie said much more softly. "I suppose I'm just spouting off scholarly facts because, to be completely honest, I'm a bit nervous about all this. I like things to be a bit more predictable. We go way back in the past, we meet a problem, we beat up the problem, we come home. Somehow it doesn't seem like that is going to be the case this time."

I took a few deep breaths to calm my nerves, smiled at my brainiac sister, and spoke in such a way that I hoped I could help calm hers as well.

"It's okay, Sis; I understand. Try not to worry; we have a constant we can lean on even when nothing else is the same."

She smiled, Aly did too, and we all quoted it out loud together.

"Hebrews 13:5, I will never leave thee, nor forsake thee."

"Let's just count on that, guys. We don't know what we're going to be facing, but we do know that our God is more than a match for whoever or whatever the owner of those red eyes is."

The girls nodded and then Aly spoke up. "So what now, Big Brother, where to?"

"I don't know yet, Squirt, I don't know. I just know that the Conductor told us that if we would go into Point Pleasant, we would find out what our mission is. We are here, I guess for now we just wait."

You know, it's funny, when you are in God's will, sometimes you may have to wait for a while, but other times the answer is almost instantaneous. It certainly was in this case, as a car came screaming by the parking lot and turned the corner on two wheels. Whoever was in that vehicle was in a major hurry to go somewhere and was driving like the devil himself was chasing him.

Aly shouted it, and we all three instantly did it; "Follow that car!"

Let me tell you, we were pedaling like madmen, or in my sisters' case, madwomen, I suppose. Fortunately, we only had to go a few blocks, because the car whipped into the police station and slammed on the brakes. Four people immediately piled out: two men and two women. The police had apparently already received a report of a maniac driver coming that way because one of them rushed out into the parking lot at the exact same moment that the four people from the car were rushing toward the door.

"Freeze!" The policeman screamed as he pulled out a gun. The four panicked passengers immediately screeched to a halt and threw their hands up. I was very glad that policeman did not have an itchy trigger finger because just a split second later one of the ladies who had stopped screamed like a banshee and lunged at his feet, wrapping herself around his legs while sobbing.

Something was very, very wrong.

We watched from the edge of the parking lot, and with as wild as the scene in front of him was, the officer never noticed us standing there.

When he spoke, it was with a decidedly firm tone of voice.

"Calm down, all of you, immediately! Pull yourselves together and tell me what in the world is going on. You have torn through the town like a tornado, and now you are screaming and wailing like you have seen a ghost. Have you been drinking? Or maybe I should ask, exactly *how much* have you been drinking?"

The light on the lamp post just overhead flickered and hummed as the sobbing woman took several seconds to try and compose herself. But it was no use. Despite her best efforts, she suddenly started sobbing again, all while maintaining her death grip on the officer's legs. Finally, one of the men spoke up.

"Officer, I know this looks bad, but you have to believe me; we haven't had so much as a drop to drink, nothing at all, I promise."

"Then what is this all about? Speak up, man, before I lock you all up for disturbing the peace."

When the answer came, it was through muffled sobs. The lady at the officer's feet was muttering into his shoes, "Eyes... red... red... they were red eyes, red... red...red..."

The look on the officer's face sent a clear message: my first guess was correct, you are all drunk.

But the look on the faces of the two men and one woman still standing sent an equally clear message: we know what we saw, and there is no amount of time that will ever make us doubt it or forget it.

Chapter Six

After what seemed like an eternity of awkward silence, but was in reality probably no longer than a minute or so, the second lady spoke up.

"Officer, I'm terribly sorry that we've caused this disturbance, you have a hard-enough job without us making it harder. It's just that, we, well, we saw something. All of us. I don't know how to say this without sounding crazy, but we saw something that, the best way I can describe it, is not of this world."

The officer looked at the woman, and his eyebrows were arched in that unmistakable "are you serious?" kind of a look. I know that look very well; both dad and mom have given it to my sisters and me more times than I care to remember.

When he spoke, to his credit, he was professional and did not assume anything.

"Okay, so you saw something. You say it was not of this world. Why don't you describe it to me, maybe I can help you all to make sense of it."

What followed, if the two couples had not been so clearly terrified, would have actually sounded hilarious. The conversation lasted maybe seven or eight minutes, and here are the things that we gleaned from it.

One, the four people were, in fact, two couples, two married couples, the Malletes and the Scarberry's. The fact that they were married young adults, and not just some crazy kids, in my mind, lent more credibility to the wild tale that they were weaving.

Two, all of the action had occurred in some place called the TNT area.

Three, whatever it was they think they saw, it could not possibly have actually been any naturally occurring thing. They basically described a huge manlike creature, nearly seven feet tall, massive wings, razor-sharp claws, and red glowing eyes. Believe me, that red eye part caught the attention of us Night Heroes, oh boy, did it ever!

Four, this was not some Big-Foot-like encounter where the best people can do is come up with a grainy video of something running away from them into the trees. These four were all adamant that whatever it is they saw was aggressive; they claimed that it chased them at up to seventy miles per hour.

By that point in their description, they were starting to get repetitive and were not saying anything new. We really didn't want to be seen or noticed, so we quietly retreated into the shadows and pedaled back to Tiny's Drive-In.

We all braked to a stop and popped the kickstands down.

"Welp," Aly said in her best southern hick voice, "that back there would sound as crazy as a bunch of drunken June bugs, except for the fact that all of us are here, and all of us have already seen those red eyes those four were babbling about."

"Drawl and all, I would have to agree with your assessment," Carrie said matter-of-factly. "We wouldn't be here if there wasn't something terribly wrong for us to deal with. And we simply cannot write off as coincidence the fact that all three of us, independently, had the exact same nightmare, which those four back there now claim to have actually seen in real life. As crazy as it sounds, it seems very much like the Lord is sending us into the 'dealing with monsters' business."

"Monsters, Sis?" I smiled as I said it, but it was mostly a smile of amazement. My ultra-logical sister actually using the word monsters? "What do you think this is, an episode of Scooby Doo?"

"Make fun if you want to, Kyle, but here's a challenge for you; can you think of a better description?"

Ouch. That hurt. Mostly because I couldn't.

"Okay then, monsters. So, what, do we go find ourselves a wooden stake or a silver bullet?"

Carrie wrinkled up her mouth to one side, which was the look she usually got on her face when she was thinking hard.

"No, no wooden stakes, no silver bullets. The description they gave was neither vampire nor werewolf. If it had been, we could safely write those people off as crazy."

"Um, Older Warner girl," Aly said, "what exactly is the difference between a vampire, a werewolf, and a seven-foot winged creature with red glowing eyes?"

"Easy answer, Younger Warner Girl, there is absolutely no evidence for the existence of vampires and werewolves. By contrast, counting us, there are apparently seven eyewitnesses to whatever this new monster is."

"Fair enough," Aly said with a shrug. "But that brings us right back around to Kyle's question, what exactly do we do with it?"

"Well, in Esther chapter two there was a report that something drastic was happening; two chamberlains were accused of plotting to kill the King. The Bible says that when that report was made, an inquisition was made of the matter. That is a fancy way of saying that they investigated what they had heard. We know what we saw in our dreams, but I am guessing that our next step is to investigate the report those two couples just made to the police and preferably to do so before the police do."

"That all sounds well and good, Miss Brainiac, but haven't you forgotten something painfully obvious?"

"And what would that be, Dear Brother?"

I placed my hands on her shoulders and scrunched down a little bit to look her in the eyes as I said it. "We have no idea where the TNT area is, every business is closed, and we can't exactly go back to the police and ask them if it is okay for us to do their job."

Her jaw dropped, she was stunned speechless.

Trust me, that doesn't happen often.

And so it was that we three hyper, all-out-all-the-time unknown heroes, ended up having to do the thing that we like the least; waiting. We knew there was nothing else that we could do for the night. We would have to use the daytime hours to find out what we could about the area, especially the TNT area.

Normally, we have to be asleep somewhere before the sun goes down so we can wake up in our time. But, since everything was flipped upside down on its head in this mission, we assumed that would have to be asleep sometime before daybreak this time around.

But where exactly were we supposed to sleep? In every previous occasion, there have been woods or forests or something along those lines for us to safely and privately bed down in. If we just went to sleep on a park bench somewhere, there is no guarantee we wouldn't be mistaken for junior vagrants and locked up, which would be an absolute disaster.

Somehow, I wasn't surprised that, in our moment of uncertainty, it was my dad who unknowingly came to the rescue.

"What does dad always say," Carrie asked?

"Um, tuck and roll?" Aly asked uncertainly.

"Not that, what does he always say about being in God's will versus being out of God's will?"

Immediately we all three said it in unison, "I would rather sleep under a bridge in the will of God than in the most comfortable mansion on earth out of the will of God."

Twenty minutes later our bikes were parked down below us, and we three Night Heroes were telling each other good night (for the second time that night) under the old Silver Bridge.

Chapter Seven

"GOOD MORNING, GOOD MORNING, GOOD MORNING, GOOD MORNING, GOOD MORNING TO YOUUUUUUUUUUUUUUUUUUUUUUUUU U!"

"Up and at 'em, sleepy heads! The day is a wasting! Up Up Up, great day for up!"

Ugh. Count on our dad to wake up A) earlier than us, B) hyper, C) chipper, and D) singing at the top of his lungs. Why, oh why could we not have been birthed into a "quiet in the morning until coffee has been consumed" kind of family?

I blinked a few times and looked over at Carrie and Aly. Amazingly, they were still curled up in their bed, not showing any indication of being awake! How do they do that?

I got up and staggered to the bathroom and started making myself presentable for the day. Sleeping under a bridge is rough on a kid.

The foam of the toothpaste gave me a distinctly rabid look. That, combined with my disheveled hair, made me glad no girls could see me right now. As I stared at myself in the mirror, I could not help but also see, somewhere in my mind, those red glowing eyes from last night and a frantic woman hugging a police officer's legs in fear.

I shook those cobwebs out of my head and finished my morning grooming rituals. I emerged from the bathroom neat, clean, and smelling vaguely Old Spice like. The girls were dressed and angling to be the next one in the bathroom. Dad was gone, I was guessing he was in the lobby scouting around for a newspaper. Mom was ironing clothes.

Thus began another "normal" day for three very abnormal kids.

Twenty minutes later we were all out the door and walking across the parking lot to the Bob Evans for breakfast. As we walked, the girls and I looked back and forth at each other, and back as well at the hotel and bridge. The knowing look on our face was sending a message our folks would never understand; "They're back!"

Dad held the door for all of us, and a moment later a nice waitress seated us all at a big booth. It did not take long for the table to be filled with pancakes, eggs, buttered toast, and breakfast steak. Man, there is nothing like the smell and taste of a good breakfast to start the day!

But dad is dad, so there would not be much sitting around time, even at a Bob Evans. We actually were out of the restaurant before others who had come in before us.

Our destination to begin the day was lovely downtown Point Pleasant. Let me tell you; this felt like the weirdest day trip ever. We were looking at every building, street name, landmark, everything, and silently comparing it with what we had seen last night. Some of the buildings were the same, with only a change of the sign out front indicating a different business altogether than what had been there in 1966. Some had been torn down somewhere along the way and replaced by newer, modern structures. I could not help but wonder if any of this would help us at all.

Dad pulled the Yukon into a cramped parking space in front of a little restaurant advertising "authentic Mexican cuisine." I knew mom and dad would be skeptical of that; mom especially is a Mexican food aficionado and knows the difference between Mexican Mexican food and American Mexican food masquerading as Mexican Mexican food.

But for the time being, with our bellies still full from our Bob Evans breakfast, Mexican food was the farthest thing from our minds, convenient parking spot notwithstanding. Dad was taking us to something he called the flood wall. He said that it had a breathtaking historical mural painted on it.

Score one for dad; he nailed this one. It was much better in the light of day. The paintings were not there when we pedaled across the bridge "last night."

Right along the riverfront of the incredibly wide Ohio River, there is a huge concrete wall bordering the city. Point Pleasant had been ravaged by floods throughout the years, especially in 1937 and 1948. Two story buildings in the downtown area had their entire bottom stories completely submerged in waters. So, by 1951, there was a flood wall around the city. I was amazed to look at the huge openings, with slots that massive inserts could be slipped into in the event of an oncoming flood.

But the wall itself also served as a tourist attraction, not just a water stopper. Not many years back, the town commissioned a famous artist to paint a mural depicting the area from its earliest days, all the way up to the present day. We walked by beautifully detailed pictures of Indians at work and play, settlers coming to the area, and the inevitable battles between them. Some of those pictures were both lovely and heartbreaking all at the same time.

Along the way, we passed gleaming silver statues of some of the historical figures painted on the wall. There was Chief Cornstalk (not kidding, that was his real name) Mad Anne Bailey (yep, her real name too, a name she earned well) and Lord Dunmore, who fought against Chief Cornstalk and his tribe.

Man, things clearly got really tense and heated back then. It would have been nice if everyone had thought a little more of others and not been so self-centered; a lot of innocent lives could have been spared.

Once the flood wall came to an end, we walked through the next yard over to what is called the Mansion House even though it is just a cabin. I suppose that description is not quite fair, though. The cabin is three stories and was situated on the riverfront, so by the standards of its day, the name probably fit pretty well.

There were a couple of men out front dressed in clothes from the Revolutionary Period. They were using old techniques to make flints for flintlock rifles. That was really, really cool. Inside the Mansion House, there is an amazing variety of old things to see: arrowheads, ancient deeds and documents, and way more.

Dad was in heaven. I could see the wheels spinning in his head, and I knew there would be some sermon illustrations coming from this.

We finished with the Mansion House, and by that time out stomachs were growling. We had actually spent three hours looking at the flood wall and through the Mansion House! History is one thing that will slow my dad down every time.

We started back down the street to the car passing the River Museum along the way. I figured there was roughly a one hundred percent chance we would end up in there before the week was over.

After another minute or so of walking, we could see the Yukon up ahead. I knew we would be stopping in at the Mexican restaurant it was parked in front of for lunch. I was already thinking of and drooling over the thought of good, sizzling fajitas. In my mind, I could already visualize them on the table.

But Aly screaming in terror snapped me out of that daydream in an instant.

Chapter Eight

As quick as a lightning bolt, dad, who had been leading the pack, had wheeled around and gotten to Aly. The look on his face was that of a man who thought one of his precious girls was in danger and was ready to kill. He scooped her up and wheeled around, looking for whatever it was that had scared her so.

Carrie was as white as a sheet and standing as stock-still as one of the statues we had seen by the river wall.

And then I saw it. Mind you, I knew in an instant that it was just a statue, but I also understood, oh boy did I understand, why Aly had screamed. For there, standing not fifteen feet away, menacingly posed, was a silver statue of a man-shaped creature with huge wings and red, glowing eyes...

And then I heard dad begin to laugh. "Seriously, sweetheart? You are screaming over a metal statue? I am pretty sure I have raised braver kids than that."

Oh dad, if you only knew! Your kids have jumped out of an airplane, fought knife-wielding Indians, and taken down a pirate. But this is something else entirely, and we don't know what, just yet.

Aly, realizing how crazy she must have looked to our parents, quickly and admirably pulled herself together and forced a laugh that I knew was not a bit genuine.

"Oh, wow, I feel so silly! That just really caught me off guard. What in the world is that thing, anyway?"

Dad laughed again and put her down. "I don't know, honey bunny, but let's check it and find out.

We made our way over to the hunk of menacing metal and checked out the plaque placed just below it:

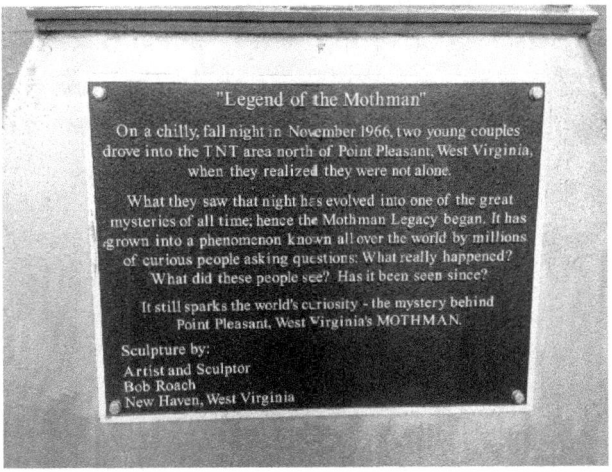

"Legend of the Mothman"

On a chilly, fall night in November 1966, two young couples drove into the TNT area north of Point Pleasant, West Virginia, when they realized they were not alone.

What they saw that night has evolved into one of the great mysteries of all time; hence the Mothman Legacy began. It has grown into a phenomenon known all over the world by millions of curious people asking questions: What really happened? What did these people see? Has it been seen since?

It still sparks the world's curiosity - the mystery behind Point Pleasant, West Virginia's MOTHMAN.

Sculpture by:
Artist and Sculptor
Bob Roach
New Haven, West Virginia

The Moth Man. Seriously? Now, I just felt ridiculous, and as I looked at Carrie and Aly, I could tell they were beginning to feel the same way. Did we really just get scared awake and yanked back in time for something this, well, nutty?

Naturally, with Dad there, we all had to pose for pictures with the statue.

But, just as naturally, it did not take him long to have us all on the move again. Before we could say, "Extra salsa, please," we were at a table saying, "Extra salsa, please."

Lunch was good. Not really authentic (never, ever argue with mom on this kind of thing. Trust me, she knows) but really good anyway. But all during the meal the girls and I were looking at each other, trying to read each other's faces to see what we each were thinking. I did not know what message my face was sending, but I was pretty sure that Carrie was saying, "We need to step back and rethink things, " and Aly was saying, "I am not looking forward to tonight."

As for me, I had enough presence of mind to remember that there was a piece of information we still desperately needed. So, the next time the waiter came through, I very politely said, "Pardon me, I have a question. Where is the TNT area?"

That did not go so well. He just looked at me blankly and said, "Sorry, I have never heard of that."

Dad was engrossed in a scoop of guacamole, but mom was paying attention and was obviously puzzled by that exchange.

"Son, what did you just ask him?"

"Oh," I replied nonchalantly, "I was asking about the TNT area. I have heard about it; it is supposed to be somewhere around here; I just don't know what or where it is. It sounded like it might be interesting."

Dad, who by that time had finished his chip of guacamole, took a drink of his tea and then said, "No one around here is likely to know where it is unless they are either an old-timer or a history buff. It hasn't been called that for a long time. It is now known as the McClintic Wildlife Area. It is a great place for hunting or fishing or camping, but back in the day it was a military and munitions area."

Now, why would I be surprised that my dad, Mr. History, would know all that?

Carrie immediately picked up on what I was doing.

"It sounds kind of cool, dad, you think we could maybe go see it while we're here?" She asked nonchalantly.

"Well, I suppose we might be able to squeeze that in, it is only six or seven miles north of town out on Route 62. I had planned on driving us into Charleston tomorrow, but we may just switch gears and go out there for a while instead. I wouldn't mind looking around."

Was I looking forward to tomorrow? No, not exactly. Mind you, I do not have anything against daytime exploring. But at the moment I was preoccupied with tonight, not tomorrow. We now knew which direction to take to get to the area where those four panicky people from last night had seen whatever it is they think they saw.

Once we finished up lunch, we went back to the hotel and dropped the girls off. Mom had some computer work she wanted to do, and both Carrie and Aly had some schoolwork they needed to finish. At the moment, I happened to be a few days ahead on my school work, so I had the privilege of going with dad to the local gym.

For my age, I am ridiculously strong. But it does not take more than a few minutes in the gym with dad for me to be reminded just how far I still have to go in that area. Watching him bench press nearly three hundred fifty pounds really lights my fire; I know one day, if I stay at it, I will be even stronger than him. And he has told me repeatedly that that is exactly what he wants.

Mom and dad both are like that. No matter what the area or field our activity is, they want the girls and me to be better at it than they have ever been. They have spent their lives pouring themselves into us, investing in us, molding us into a boy and two girls who will one day be godly adults, equipped to serve the Lord in every imaginable way.

If only they knew how much we are already serving!

A sweaty hour and a half later we were making our way back to the car and then back to the hotel. The businesses whipped past the windows on both sides like frantic memories of red eyes in the night. I shut my eyes tightly as if to suppress the memory and breathed in and out a few times deeply, and all the way to the hotel prayed one more time to the God who knows and cares.

The atmosphere in the hotel room was pretty quickly full of powder and hairspray and makeup. I declare, I don't think any insects could even survive the lovely fumigation the Warner women subject us all to.

Soon enough, though, I was breathing the far more healthy oxygen in the hallway leading to the lobby and then the outdoor air leading to the Yukon. Five buckles quickly clicked, and with an easy turn of the switch, the Yukon roared to life once again. Several happy, noisy minutes later, we pulled into the parking lot of the Jordan Baptist Church for the second night of the meeting.

Church is such an amazing thing; I cannot imagine why anyone wouldn't like it. The same people who shook hands and smiled and clapped each other on the back last night did it all over again on this night as if they had not seen each other in years and were so happy to be together again.

We were wrapped up all in the middle of it. Folks from another state and another town, and yet we were treated like we were home among family.

And I guess in reality we were. Galatians 6:10 calls Christians the "household of faith." We are brothers and sisters to a whole lot of people we know well, a whole lot of others we just barely know, and yet others that we have not yet even met.

How cool is that?

The service started promptly at seven o'clock with the song leader leading the congregation in a rousing few verses of Victory in Jesus. When We All Get to Heaven came next, and as soon as the last victoryyyyyy had faded, Pastor Burgess stood to welcome everyone.

The next twenty minutes were a wonderful whirlwind of announcements, offering, special songs, and people testifying of the goodness of God.

Then it was time for the best part of any service, the preaching of God's word.

Dad had everyone open their Bibles to Romans 8:28. It is one of the most amazing promises in the entire Bible. It says, "And we know that all things work together for good to them that love God, to them who are the called according to his purpose."

God never said all things were good; that would be ridiculous and untrue. He did say that for Christians who love Him, all things *work together* for good. God takes all of the things in our lives, even the horrible things, and mixes them with other ingredients in our lives and produces something fantastic.

The illustration my dad always uses in this message is about air. He says, "Argon and Carbon Dioxide are very bad. Very, very bad. If you were in a room of nothing but Argon and Carbon Dioxide, you would die pretty quickly. Nitrogen, on the other hand, is inert. It is basically a whole lot like nothingness. If you were in a room full of nothing but Nitrogen, you would once again die pretty quickly, because while it is not technically bad for you, it also contains nothing that is good for you, nothing that your body can use. Pure Oxygen is ok, for a little while, but if you were in a room of pure oxygen, you would still die in a matter of a couple of weeks from the very nasty effects of Oxygen poisoning. But if you mix 78% Nitrogen, 21% Oxygen, and 1% Argon and Carbon Dioxide, do you know what you get? You get to breathe because all of these ingredients make up our air."

What a God, Who can take even the things that the devil intended to destroy us and make good things come out of them!

The service ended way too soon, as it always does, and we were headed out for another hour or so of fellowship. On this night we made our way into Gallipolis, Ohio, to the

Pip and Huds Yogurt Shop with the pastors and their families. It is a lot like a Sweet Frog from back home. Really, really good. Did you know that M&Ms, blackberries, sprinkles, and marshmallows can all be crammed together onto a huge dollop of yogurt?

Yep, that would be Aly.

We had a great time, got thoroughly sugared up, and soon were heading back toward the hotel. Aly was bouncing off of the walls of the vehicle. If a sugar rush could be carried into the past, I suspected some red-eyed creature was about to meet his match tonight in the form of a blonde-headed hyper pixie.

Chapter Nine

I was crashing through the limbs and weeds, heart racing and about to pound out of my chest. The wet branches were slapping me in the face bidding me to slow down or stop, but the nameless terror behind me was propelling me forward. I felt like I could not breathe, but I dared not stop. I could hear it getting closer, hissing my name, Kyyyyyyyyle, Kyyyyyyyyle!

"Kyle! Wake up!"

I lunged upward off of my floor mat, and just barely stifled back a scream. Carrie and Aly were beside me, looking intently into my panicked eyes. Carrie spoke again.

"Settle down, Big Brother, you're safe. We are still in the hotel room."

My eyes scanned the room frantically, adjusting to the darkness.

Aly spoke softly, "Apparently it is all on you tonight. Neither Carrie or I had the nightmare. No red eyes for us."

I willed my heart to stop racing and forced my breathing to slow.

"Wow, that was rough. That is the most life-like nightmare I have ever have. That thing was all up on me, and no matter how fast I ran, I couldn't get away."

We sat there in the darkness for a few silent moments, giving me time to compose myself. I knew what we had to do; I just didn't want to. Finally, Carrie said it.

"We have to go, Y'all, the night is wasting."

I dropped my head and shook out the cobwebs, then raised it back up and smiled a brave smile that I did not feel. A few seconds later we were quietly leaving the room once again. Mom and dad were sound asleep. I could not help but wonder if God was doing for them what He did for Adam, placing them into a deep sleep until His work was done.

We made our way down the dim hallway and toward the entrance of the hotel. Honestly, it almost looked like some sinister, otherworldly fog that we were walking through. We made our way out into the parking lot, and there was the Conductor standing with his back to us once more. We made our way to him, and then as if on cue, turned around to look.

The hotel and bridge were gone once again. Hello, 1966.

"So, Night Heroes, how has your trip been so far? Sleeping well?"

He said this with a wry smile. I was not feeling the humor at the moment.

"Now that you mention it, no, not really. To quote Ebenezer Scrooge, 'an uninterrupted night's rest might aid my welfare.'"

"I suppose it would, but only in the short term, Kyle. What will really aid your welfare is confronting and overcoming the problem at hand."

"Yes, Sir," I said in much less of a cross mood, "I suppose it would."

He smiled that kind smile and responded, "TNT Area tonight?"

We all nodded in silent unanimity.

"Good choice, I would think. Be safe as you travel, and Godspeed to you all."

Be safe as you travel, he said. That would require help from the only One who can truly grant safety, and we knew it. And so once again we three Warner kids knelt and approached the throne of the all-knowing God and asked Him to give us safety as we faced the unknown.

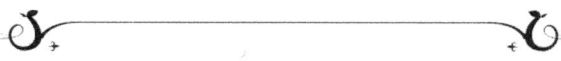

From the place we were now standing to the TNT area would be a ride of about eleven miles for us. With our top-of-the-line, brand new to 1966 antique bikes, that would take us about thirty-five or forty minutes, I was guessing.

"Welp, guess we better push pedals, Y'all."

I grinned at Aly and shook my head in amusement. "You are really getting into this drawl thing, Sis."

She just grinned back. "Then let me say this plainly enough for you to understand it, Kyle; try and keep up."

And with that, she turned right and was off like a shot, with Carrie hot on her back wheel, and me keeping pace a bike length behind.

About a mile later, we turned right onto the Silver Bridge and started climbing. At the top, Aly, still in the lead, abruptly stopped, and Carrie and I pulled up along either side of her.

"What's up, Munchkin? Getting tired?"

Normally a quip like that would have brought out the claws. But Aly just sat there in quiet contemplation for another second or two, and then answered thoughtfully.

"No. I'm just thinking about the fact that a year from now this very bridge will collapse, taking forty-six people unexpectedly to their deaths. I wonder how many of their driveways we will be passing right by these next few days."

"That, Littlest Sister, is exactly why every person should be saved and ready to meet God at any moment. James 4:14 says, 'Whereas ye know not what shall be on the morrow. For what is your life? It is even a vapour, that appeareth for a little time, and then vanisheth away.'"

We sat there in silence for a few moments, watching the water below, and thinking our own thoughts. Then as if by a silent call, we all started pedaling again.

We cruised easily down the other side of the bridge, which ran right over top of the flood wall in Point Pleasant that we had looked at this afternoon.

Once we bottomed out, we turned left onto Viand Street and kept pedaling. The shuttered-for-the-day businesses on both sides of the road clipped by us at a regular pace. Soon there were fewer and fewer of those, especially after we rounded the curve in Point Pleasant and started heading out of town on Route 62. After that first mad dash, we kept a fairly steady and sustainable pace as town gave way to fields.

The night was cold, and the sweat from our exertion on the bikes only made it more so. The wind whistling threateningly through the trees added yet another layer to the chill.

I reached into my pocket and pulled out a small LED flashlight, clicked it on and put it in my mouth, and quickly shot around Carrie and Aly. Leading the way while drooling on that flashlight, we soon pulled up to a sign that said "Point Pleasant Ordnance Works," and we coasted to a stop.

"Well, here we are, guys, the TNT Area. So, what say you, Little Sister and Littler Sister, shall we cruise down the spooky dirt road and have a look see or shall we turn around and go back?"

I knew the reaction that would garner. Sure enough, both of them glared at me.

"If you want to go all poultry on us, Chicken Boy, help yourself," Carrie snapped. "Aly and I can surely handle the imaginary monster from here."

"Imaginary?" I queried. "How have we leaped to that conclusion? We all woke up to red eyes in the night, and we all saw those frightened couples babbling at the police station. As of last night, you were all on board with the 'monster' theory. What gives?"

"Come on, Kyle, you saw that statue. This is some kind of a ploy to drum up the tourist business, and apparently, it worked better than the originator's wildest dreams. People in the twenty-first century are still coming to town and buying t-shirts, key chains, and little Moth-Man statues. I don't know what is out here, but I suspect we have been sent to deal with mischief makers rather than monsters."

Aly was shaking her head fiercely while Carrie spoke.

"No, Sis, just no. This is way more than a human mischief maker. Please don't take this so lightly; I have a really bad feeling about it."

Carrie's face softened. No matter what her giant intellect told her, her heart for her sister was still bigger than her brain.

"Okay, Aly, I'll keep an open mind, and all of us will keep open eyes. Deal?"

"Deal," Aly said as she smiled in obvious relief.

We turned in and began to pedal, and I could not help but notice how slowly and quietly all three of us were going.

The gravel crunched under our tires, and I was once again out front with my LED light in my mouth. I did not really know what we were looking for or where to look. I did know, after a solid ten minutes of pedaling, that the area was huge. There were side roads shooting off of the main road, and the main road seemed to never end.

Finally, I slowed to a stop, and the girls joined me. I knew by now that we were going to have to examine the side roads if we expected to find anything.

"Guys, we are not getting anywhere fast this way."

"Ya think?" Carrie quipped.

"I do. I would say we are going to have to start branching off down these side roads and see what we can find."

I saw Aly's eyes widen.

"Seriously? In other words, leave the really creepy dirt road in favor of one of the really ultra super duper creepy paths that come off of the really creepy dirt road?"

I wrinkled my face up trying to absorb all that, then said, "I suppose you could put it that way. I would tend to put it more like, 'let's not waste all night pedaling down the road with nothing on it.'"

The look on Aly's face told me that we were about to engage in a lengthy back-and-forth on this one.

"Look, Bro, I am all in favor of..."

And that was as far as she got. That was as far as any of us got. The blood-curdling scream in the distance ended any conversation on our part for the moment and sent us scurrying for the cover of the trees, bikes and all.

Chapter Ten

My heart felt like it was about to beat out of my chest; I was guessing that Carrie and Aly were experiencing the same thing. For what seemed like an eternity, we sat there trying to gather our wits while simultaneously trying to be as silent as the grave.

No, I do not miss the irony of that last statement.

"Okay, guys," I whispered, "it appears to me that we have three choices. We can sit here quietly, go to sleep, and get our nightly ride home, we can ride quietly away and then once we hit the road pedal like the devil himself is chasing us, or we can be completely insane and start moving in the direction of that bloodcurdling scream to investigate."

Three options, one of which made no sense to me whatsoever. But somehow, I just knew how this was going to go.

"Are we Night Heroes or Night Zeroes?" Aly asked with a mixture of fear and anger. "Someone out there is clearly in trouble, and I rather suspect that there is no one around other than us who can or will help."

Carrie, for her part, looked frustrated. Scared, yes, but mostly frustrated. I knew her well enough to know that the only time that particular look is on her face is when she does not understand something.

"My brain is telling me we have nothing to worry about. We know that there are no such things as monsters. The evidence we have thus far tells me that someone or someones are messing with us. But that scream sounded awfully genuine. I would love to pack it in and ride away right now, but I don't want to live with the irritation of not finding out what is going on. I say we investigate."

Two votes for going toward the sound of the scream. Why couldn't I have chicken girls for sisters?

"Okay, we go investigate. But that brings up another question. Which direction do we go? Are we confident we know where the scream came from?"

Carrie closed her eyes as if thinking and said, "Well, let's see if we are all on the same page on this one. So that none of us will be influenced by the others, you guys do what I have done and close your eyes tight. At the count of three, everyone point in the direction that you believe the scream came from. Then at the count of three, we will all open our eyes and see if we have a good idea which way we should go."

She breathed in and out slowly and said, "One... Two... Three."

I heard three arms go up.

One more time Carrie breathed in and out and said, "One... Two... Three."

We opened our eyes, and I sucked in my breath. Every last one of us was pointing the exact same direction.

I heard my voice say "awesome" in a tone of voice that said, "oh great..."

"Yep," Aly said with a grin, "straight down the spooky path into the dark woods. When the story of our life is written, that will probably be the theme of it."

"Let's just hope we live long enough to be able to laugh about that," I said with a slow shake of my head.

And with that, without even having to discuss it, we silently fell into our normal order, me up front, Aly in the middle, Carrie in the back, and prayers going silently upward as we quietly crept into the unknown.

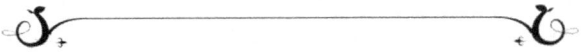

It is almost hard to accurately describe just how eerie the TNT Area of 1966 was in the darkness of night. Part of this was due to the way it was designed to begin with. Since its purpose was the manufacture and storage of explosives for the war effort, the people who made it decided that both safety and camouflage needed to be part of the equation. As we passed in utter silence along the trail, I was amazed at how very "normal" this place would have seemed from the air.

"Check it out," I hissed at the girls, as I let my light fall on a metal door that seemed to be coming out of the side of a hill. Instinctively we crouched down and got on our knees and stayed there, stock still, evaluating the situation.

"What is that, Kyle?"

It was Aly that asked, but Carrie answered before I could.

"If I didn't know better I would think that would be a hobbit hole."

Count on our resident Lord of the Rings fan to come up with that one.

"Not unless the hobbits around here are very much normal size," I responded. "I'm guessing that that metal door doesn't lead into a cozy warm living room with cheese and butter and bread, but into a concrete bunker that once held dynamite. The fact that it is covered in dirt and grass and trees is a sign of the sheer geniusery of the people who made it. Any spy planes or satellites who were staring down at it from above would think it was just part of the naturally hilly terrain of West Virginia."

"You think that could be where our scream came from?" Aly asked hesitantly.

"I don't know, sis, but I suppose there is one way we can find out."

No one moved, and no one spoke. For several seconds it was as if we all knew we needed to go up to and past that creepy metal door and into that ominous bunker, but no one wanted to take the first step.

Well, as dad would say, "God made you a man for a reason, Kyle. So act like it."

I slowly rose from my kneeling position and begin to take the quietest, Apache-like steps I could take off of the pathway and toward that metal door. I could not hear them behind me, but I knew my lionhearted sisters well enough to know that I did not even need to look back; they were right there with me.

After what seemed like an eternity we had covered the thirty feet or so to the door. Everyone had stopped breathing and was listening intently for any sound that might warn us of impending danger.

There was nothing.

Oh so slowly, I eased my flashlight around the door and shined it in the pitch black tomb-like darkness of the bunker.

Again, there was nothing.

Still barely breathing, I took a step into the enclosure, and then another, and then another. Finally, I was in the center of it all, with Carrie and Aly beside me. It looked like the hugest, most perfect igloo ever built, except for the fact that it was made of concrete instead of snow and ice.

And that is when I said one word that instantly became dozens:

"Wow wow wow wow wow wow wow wow wow wow wow wow wow..."

All of our faces went ashen white with a look of sheer horror and panic. How could I not have known this would happen! The floor was concrete, the entire structure was concrete, it was perfectly round, any sound was going to echo like a golf ball being driven into a tile bathroom.

Instantly we whirled around and ran for the opening. We bolted past it and kept going straight back into the woods and baseball slid up under some nearby bushes of unknown identity. At that moment none of us cared if it was poison ivy! We knew that anyone nearby was now alerted to our presence, and we did not want to get caught by whomever it was or whatever it was that caused that blood-curdling scream. I especially did not want to get caught in that bunker. If someone had slammed that steel door shut behind us, we would never escape and never be found until the day of the rapture.

It had to be at least a half an hour that we lay there breathing shallowly without saying a word. Finally, it seemed like it might be safe enough to whisper.

"Well, dad always said that once a word comes out of your mouth is just like a bullet out of a gun; you can't get it back. That 'wow' is one word I would sure like to have back."

"No joke, Kyle," Carrie said in amazement. "I don't think the trumpet of the Lord could get any more attention than that. So, what now?"

"Well, I hate to say it, but for the night, I would say we are beaten. We have absolutely lost any element of surprise. Whoever or whatever is out there now knows that we are out here too. And they or it have a particularly insurmountable advantage over us at this moment; they know the area, and we are poking around in the darkness. I say for tonight we beat a retreat. Let's do everything we can to get dad to bring us out here tomorrow so that we can look around during the daytime and get a better sense of the area that we are dealing with. That way when we come back tomorrow night we can be fighting on a little more level playing field."

There was no argument from either of my sisters on that, none whatsoever. We re-gathered our metallic steeds and started pedaling back to our temporary nighttime home. I knew that right now, a thirty-five-minute ride would calm our nerves and do us good.

Chapter Eleven

"Good grief, do all guys drool like that?"

My left eye blinked open just a little bit as my mind began to process the voice. It took me a second, but I finally settled on that of my littlest sister. That thought was confirmed for me a second later when Carrie answered her.

"Of course, they do, Aly, it is one of the many non-endearing traits of the masculine gender."

She must have said that where dad could hear it, and he apparently gave her the "dad look," because she quickly pivoted to a good verbal save, "Other than dad, of course; he is way too cool to drool."

Too cool to drool. Dad was belly laughing at that, and I knew I would hear that statement repeatedly for a good while.

And then I felt the moist spot on my cheek. Apparently, I was the drooler they were talking about. Good grief.

I yawned and rolled over to the dry side of the pillow.

"Get up, Kyle," mom said sweetly but firmly. And, since the only thing that makes dad angrier than having kids disobey him is having kids disobey mom, I quickly sat up and dropped my feet onto the floor with the rest of me following.

Thus began the wonderful Warner morning ritual of showering and poofing and primping and dressing and preparing to make ourselves presentable to the world at large.

Moments later we were heading out the door to the trusty old Yukon to go in search of some breakfast. Dad was in one of his "life is too short to be normal" moods, so Bob Evans was not on the menu for today. One of the things he has taught us is that when you go somewhere, be sure and find the little local diners where people eat and eat there. Some of the greatest places we have ever eaten have been the little out of the way hole-in-the-wall joints that serve some of the best food the world will never know about.

We made our way into Point Pleasant and passed a cute little place that said "Café." Dad somewhat haphazardly shoved on the brakes, whipped into a parking lot, and turned around. "Café it is," I mumbled happily under my breath.

Thirty seconds later we were parked and unloading. I had to admit that I found it a bit odd that the parking lot was mostly empty for that particular time of the morning. I hoped that was not an indication of the quality of the food.

Dad got to the door with all of us behind him and tugged on the handle. Surprisingly, it was locked. but even more surprisingly, a split second later we heard the buzzing sound and the lock lifting, allowing us to open the door. In all of my lifetime, I have never been in a restaurant that had security doors where you had to be buzzed in to enter. I could tell by the puzzled look on dad's face that he was just as surprised as I was.

And then we had another security door to go through. What in the world was this food made of, gold?

Once we entered, though, the surprises just kept coming.

There were no tables in the dining room.

There was, however, a lady behind the counter looking at us in a manner that said, "You don't get it, do you?"

"This is a gambling establishment," she said dryly.

Yikes! Double yikes!! I cannot tell you how fast we got out of there. Every one of us was red in the face, dad most of all.

But by the time we got back in the vehicle he was laughing hysterically and all of the rest of us along with him. We are the only family I know that constantly manages to get ourselves into messes like that. I could just see some photographer out front managing to snap a picture of us and plastering our faces all over the front page of newspapers everywhere, with a giant headline, "EVANGELIST AND FAMILY ENJOY GAMBLING OUTING."

When we finally stopped laughing, dad said, "Well, apparently the word Café does not mean the same thing everywhere you go. What say we find something a bit more predictable for breakfast, shall we?"

And so, three or four miles later we stopped at the Tudor's Biscuit World. May I make a recommendation to you? If you ever happen to be anywhere and see one of those, stop and eat. They truly have some of the best biscuits I have ever eaten, and my biscuit of choice that morning was a chicken, egg, and cheese biscuit. I am pretty sure that will be one of the fruits on the tree of life in heaven.

As we sat down over the biscuits and home fries, Dad said, "So, what do you guys want to do today?"

All of us knew the answer to that one instantly. We also knew better than to overplay our hand and all speak at once. There is nothing good that can come from acting weird and suspicious, especially around someone as sharp as my dad.

Carrie, our resident genius, was the right one to handle this.

"Would it be okay if we go and see that wildlife area you were talking about yesterday, the one that used to be called the TNT area? It sounds really interesting."

Dad swallowed his bite of biscuit, washed it down with some unsweet tea, and said, "Sure, that will be a great idea, I think. In fact, we can go right after we are finished breakfast since it is only a few miles from here."

This was going to be great. I really cannot overemphasize that enough; this was going to be GREAT. Great as in, "We get to see the creepy place in the daytime when it will not be so creepy, and there will not be people screaming, and we will not be running and diving under bushes because we have just alerted who knows what to our presence."

We finished up our breakfast, and dad spent a moment handing a gentleman a gospel track and inviting him to come out for the revival meeting. Then we loaded up into the Yukon, let two pick-up trucks and a tractor go by, turned right out of the parking lot and headed out for our daytime adventure.

Chapter Twelve

Seeing the fields and scenery go by in the daytime was sort of surreal. We had pedaled these very roads at night more than 50 years earlier, even though we are only teenagers. Much of it looked the same, but I could see one enormous difference in the distance, a huge power plant that had clearly been built sometime after the 60s.

By car it only took us three or four minutes from town to get to the area we had been in last night. But, where last night there had been a fairly well-kept looking sign advertising the ordnance area, by daylight and in the modern time that sign was gone, and a far less impressive looking one had taken its place. I took this picture of it mostly because I am amazed at how disrespectful people can be in spraying their stinking graffiti over everything that does not belong to them:

The red paint on the sign had faded through the years, and weathering had taken its toll, and then the artwork of the "spray paint Rembrandt" had been the final touch in the sign's decay. But as we made our way into the area, it was clear that the sign was not the only thing that had deteriorated over the years both by nature and neglect and also humanity.

"This place is way overgrown," Carrie whispered quietly to me. "I would honestly have expected things to be clearer and more well-kept than what we saw last night, but the opposite appears to be true."

I just nodded in agreement with her.

The McClintic wildlife area, in the light of day, proved to be huge. There is a central dirt and gravel road that runs through it, and dad drove all the way to the end of it. It took 15 minutes at least. The entire time we drove, while Aly and I were looking out of the windows, Carrie was doodling on a piece of paper. Why does my sister have to be off in her own little world like that when we are seeing cool things?

"Really, Sis?" I whispered.

She ignored me and continued doodling and periodically looking up and then going back to her doodling.

"Well," dad said with some consternation, "it appears that on the main road, nothing is actually all there is to see. I would suggest therefore that we go back closer to the beginning and explore some of those side paths that come off of it."

We Night Heroes cut our eyes to each other and had a silent message passing between us; "We have been on one of those side paths. We know what is there."

We bumped back down the gravel road, passing the occasional fisherman parked on the side by the creek. When we got back more towards the main area, we started paying attention to the little path that branched off on either side.

"Check it out, you guys," Aly whispered as she wrinkled up her face, "all of those paths are overgrown, but they are laid out as symmetrical as a tic-tac-toe board."

Sure enough, she was right. They were at exact intervals and distances. Being as how it was a military complex back in the day, that made sense. As we passed them by now, there was a rope or a fence or some type of barrier across the way for each one. Vehicles were clearly not allowed down those roads, but the footpath that passed by all of the barriers told us that it was very normal and expected for people to walk them.

Since all of them looked the exact same, there was no real rhyme or reason as to which one we would stop at. Dad seemed to know this, and so he finally just stopped at a place where the Yukon would be out of the way of other traffic.

"Okay, Warner wife and Warner brats, if we are going to explore, this would be as good a place as any. So, fall out, but when you get near the water, of which there is plenty out there, don't fall in."

We locked up the vehicle, crossed the gravel road, and made our way up to this decrepit metal gate:

"Things around here are not very well kept, are they?" mom said to no one in particular.

"No, but that makes it that much cooler," dad said with a smile. "Let's go explore."

I honestly did not know if this was the particular pathway we had been on last night. Things tend to look so much different in the daytime when one is not terrified. But it began to be very clear to me as I consider the symmetry of the layout that every single pathway was going to be pretty much identical, and the placement of every storage unit would be equally identical.

You know, last night it really felt like we had gone a mile down the trail in the darkness before we came on that first storage unit. I felt pretty silly in the light of day as I realized it had only been a hundred yards or so. But I also felt a tingling, horrifying sensation crawling up my spine as I looked in the light of day at the very same kind of metal door that we, in our minds, so nearly got trapped behind last night.

"Here it is, guys, the first igloo!" Dad said excitedly.

"Igloo? Is that really what they are called?"

"It is, Aly, yes. Come on inside you will see why."

I already knew.

We five walked in, and I have to say that in the daytime, it was much more cool than creepy. It actually did look like a perfect huge concrete igloo. It was built in sixteen sections and was about forty-five feet from one side to the other. No one had said anything as of yet, and dad waved his hand at us to get our attention. He put his finger to his lips in the universal "be quiet" symbol. Then he put his middle finger and thumb together, and I knew what was about to happen.

SNAP snap snap snap snap snap snap snap snap snap...

It sounded like a machine gun had gone off. If a person were to shout in a place like this, it would be deafening. Or, I thought if a person were for some reason to scream...

I looked over at Carrie and Aly and could tell they were thinking the exact same thing.

For the next two hours, we wandered from igloo to igloo, down one pathway after another. That area has some amazing natural beauty. Here is a picture of one of the ponds out there:

As we went in and out of the igloos, we were time and again confronted by the first thing that made me angry when I came into the wildlife area, graffiti. Why can people not seem to understand that they are damaging property that does not belong to them? Our parents taught us better. I promise you, if my dad ever found out that we had defaced public property, he would have put some of his own marks with a paddle on the backside of our private property.

Here is a picture of one of the more telling pieces of graffiti:

Now, as near as I can figure it if Gage actually wrote that himself, there are only two options here. Either Gage has a girlfriend with a really weird name, (Do you, Gage, take Weed to be your lawful wedded wife, to prune and to trim...) Or Gage smokes marijuana, in which case Gage is likely to spend most of his life unemployed.

But it was in the very next igloo we went to that we came across some graffiti that led to a clue about what we may be facing. I will not show the picture here because I do not want to glorify either evil or stupidity. But the picture was of a pentagram, a five-pointed satanic star, spray-painted on the wall.

"Check it out, Dad," Carrie said disgustedly. "Who in the world be so stupid as to worship the devil?"

"Some people certainly are," dad said offhandedly, "but whoever did that is just the stupid part without the devil worshiper part."

That caught my attention.

"What do you mean, Dad?"

"It is right side up," he said. "A true Satan worshiper would know enough to have it turned with the point down. Whoever did this is an ignorant wannabe, a pretender with a $.99 can of blue paint. This, though..."

His voice trailed off, as he made his way to the very center of the room. He knelt down on one knee and began to brush a light coat of dust away. Then he got down on all fours, took a long breath, and blew the rest of the fine dust away. When he did, all of the rest of us sucked in our breath.

"This is old," he said, "decades-old. And utterly genuine."

It was so perfect it looked like it could have been carved by machine. A perfectly sized pentagram.

"The bottom point is facing exactly south," dad said, "and it is sized and oriented correctly. Whoever did this was the real deal. And check out the staining in it; sometime a very long time ago blood was shed right here."

We Night Heroes have faced so much, but I have never had a colder feeling run up my back than I did that moment.

And then the most unexpected thing happened. Right there beside the spot where devil worshipers had plied their trade so very long ago, my dad began to pray to Someone much greater.

"Lord God," he said as if his heart was breaking, "I do not know what person or persons did this. I do not know if they are still alive or if they went out into eternity to meet You long ago. I do know that You love them and that You died for them, and that they, like those who crucified you, 'know not what they do.' Father, if they are still alive somewhere and walking this earth, and they do not yet know You as their God, and they do not yet know your Son as their Savior, I pray that they will come to know You before it is too late.

"No one is beyond your reach, Lord, I know that. We cannot change the past, but You can certainly change their future. I pray all this in the lovely name of Jesus, amen."

As we left that igloo heading back for the Yukon my dad's prayer was still echoing in my ears. Especially the part where he said, "we cannot change the past..."

Oh, dad, if only you knew!

Chapter Thirteen

Do you remember earlier when I said there was just about a one hundred percent chance we would end up at the River Museum before the week was out? That is, of course, the very next spot we ended up.

If you ever get a chance, I highly recommend it, if for no other reason, the fact that upstairs there is a huge interactive display that allows you to virtually pilot boats along the river. That may well be one of the coolest things ever.

We spent a couple of hours going through all of the displays and reading all of the information. I may be young, but I never get tired of going to museums. A learning person is a growing person.

That said, though, a growing person can become a growling person at some point, especially when that person is hungry. I was that growling person at the moment, but I was also starting to get pretty excited about what that meant. Today we would be meeting pastor Burgess at one of the most unique eating places you will ever find anywhere in the world, Hillbilly Hotdogs.

About thirty miles outside of Point Pleasant is a place that is really too small to be called a town, Lesage, West Virginia. Like everywhere else in West Virginia it is incredibly beautiful and so far out of the way that most of the world will never see it. As we made our way there and the lovely scenery whooshed by our windows, I began to muse over the paradox that is the American hotdog. There is no hot dog creature that the hot dog comes from; it is a mishmash of mystery meat. And yet, when placed on a soft white flour bun and generously covered with ketchup and mustard and pickles and onions and jalapenos and slaw it becomes the nearest thing to heavenly manna most of us will ever eat this side of Glory.

As we pulled into the parking lot, I heard Carrie say, "Whoa!" Whoa as in, "Is this really an eating place?"

How exactly do you describe what you see at Hillbilly Hotdogs? I suppose you could start with the rusted white passenger van that has somehow been mounted in the top of the tree. Or you could start with the outhouses, or the giant moonshine still that has been converted to a decorative water fountain, or all of the "hillbilly artifacts." But really, the most interesting visual part of Hillbilly Hotdogs is the dining room.

The dining room at Hillbilly Hotdogs is two old yellow school buses that have been hooked together and air-conditioned. All of the original school bus seats are there, and tables have been placed between them to eat on. There is not a square inch of the place anywhere that does not have someone's name drawn on it in black magic marker. And unlike the graffiti we saw at the TNT area, this is actually encouraged by the owners.

The menu features a wide assortment of food other than hotdogs. This was good since my mom is allergic to anything that has pork in it. She got a hamburger that looked truly amazing, and all the rest of us got some of the various creative hotdogs they have to offer.

None of us, though, were brave enough to try the home wrecker. That particular item is a behemoth with a two-pound hotdog covered with four pounds of toppings. It costs $20, but if you can eat it all in fifteen minutes, it is free. Free, except of course for the hospital bill that would surely follow. That you would have to pay for yourself...

We all left there an hour later stuffed like little pigs. We had laughed and cut up and had an excellent time of fellowship with pastor

Burgess and his dear wife, but now it was time to go back to the hotel and get ready for the most important part of the day. Yes, the preaching was even more important that whatever adventure we would be on during the nighttime hours that followed. Nothing, nothing anywhere ever, anytime is more important than the preaching of God's word. Paul said in 1 Corinthians 1:21 that "It pleased God by the foolishness of preaching to save them that believe." We three kids may be Night Heroes, but people like my dad that spend their lives every day and night preaching the gospel are greater heroes still.

The service that night was excellent. Both Pastor Burgess and Pastor Pinson have such a burden for their own people and for the lost. Dad preached a message from Revelation 5 called "Unworthy." It is amazing to think that in all the universe there was only one person found worthy to open the book, that is the Lord Jesus Christ. Even old beloved John the Apostle himself, the apostle Jesus loved, was not worthy to open the book.

The entire point of the message, if I understand it right, is that if we expect to be worthy before God, we need to understand that we will never accomplish it on our own. The only way we can ever be worthy is to receive the righteousness of Christ. When a sinner repents of his sin and gives himself to Jesus, the righteousness of Christ is added to his account. The Bible word for that is "imputed." When Jesus died, He took all of my sins and put it on His account. When I got saved, He took all of His righteousness and put it on my account. How amazing is that?

Apparently, I am not the only one that thinks so, because that very night two people came to the altar and repented of their sins and with tears streaming down their cheeks asked Jesus to save them. Man, I love it when that happens! It makes me feel like I could fight the devil himself.

That very thought ran through my mind, and just a split second later I regretted the fact that it did because I suddenly got a picture in my head of evil red eyes staring at me.

I shuddered just a little bit, and mom must have noticed. She slipped her arm around me and said, "I love you, Son."

That's my mom. Without even knowing what I'm going through, she knows exactly what to say to make it better.

The service ended with happy tears all around, and soon everyone was saying goodbye for the night. Dad had that happy look on his face that he gets every single time someone gets saved as a result of his preaching. He knows that all the credit belongs to God, but he is just thrilled that God chose to use him in the process.

Yep, there is no way around it; I have the best family in the world.

And that is the same happy thought that I was still thinking half an hour later when I drifted off peacefully to sleep.

Chapter Fourteen

I was frantically shaking Aly trying to get her awake before she woke mom and dad up. I knew what must be going on in her dream as she cried and whimpered and shook.

"C'mon, Sis, wake up!" I hissed.

She kept crying and kept whimpering and was getting louder and louder. Carrie woke up in a panic and immediately realized what was going on, and she joined in to help me.

"Aly! Aly! Wake up right now!"

With one of the loudest gasps I have ever heard, she sat straight up in bed, and I immediately clamped my hand over her mouth and then pulled her to my chest."

"Shhhhhh, Sis, it's okay; I've got you. You're safe."

She stopped struggling and just melted into my arms as she cried. Carrie was stroking her on the head and back, whispering words of comfort to her.

Finally, after several minutes, her crying subsided, and she began to breathe normally. But I knew that was not what I needed to be watching for to determine when she was ready.

And then she began to stiffen up, and I actually felt her jaw clench up as she laid against my chest.

"Atta girl, that's more like it," I grinned.

"So help me, Y'all, I am going to claw this monster's evil red eyeballs out when I get ahold of it."

Now that is what I needed to hear.

"Good, Sis, good. Just keep that thought front and center in your mind."

I looked over at Carrie, and she had almost a blank look on her face. Almost, except for that tinge of concern, she was clearly feeling for her baby sister.

"What's up, Carrie, what is going through that big brain of yours?"

"Nothing, Kyle, let's just go ahead and get to the business at hand."

She said "nothing," but I knew that "nothing" really meant something. And I had a pretty good idea I knew what it was. Aly and I were very much sold on the reality of whatever this thing was that we were facing. Carrie, who for some reason had not been singled out for one of these dreams like Aly and I had, was seriously doubting the dream that we all three had on the very first night.

I didn't say anything to her, but I knew that could be a problem at some point. Jesus said that a house divided against itself cannot stand; I knew that exact same truth applied to a team as well, especially a team like the Night Heroes. Everything we had ever been sent to accomplish had been predicated on us acting together as a unified trio. I feared what may happen if we went into something like this with the slightest fracture between us.

Without a word, we all slipped out of the room and into the eerie hallway once again. A moment later we were walking into the parking lot, and we did not even have to look back to know that the hotel and the Silver Memorial Bridge were gone once again.

There, as always, was the Conductor waiting for us.

"Good evening, Night Heroes," he said as we slipped up beside him. "It seems that storm clouds are gathering, doesn't it?"

We all looked up into the sky, and I am sure our faces must have wrinkled in confusion as we beheld the wondrous beauty of trillions of stars against the black velvet of night with nary a cloud to be found covering them anywhere.

"No, children," he said in answer to the question that we had not uttered, "not that kind of storm clouds."

I understood. I was guessing that Carrie and Aly did as well.

"Yes sir, it surely does. This is not like any danger that we have faced before, nor do we have the advantage of the daylight, and I have a very bad feeling based on what we had found on the floor of that TNT bunker today."

The Conductor continued to stand staring off into the distance, but I could see the almost imperceptible movement of him nodding his head in agreement.

"So, what is your plan for the night?"

"Well..."

It was at that moment that Carrie very uncharacteristically interrupted me. My sister is almost never rude, so the word uncharacteristically, believe me, applied.

"I suggest we go back into Point Pleasant to the police station and see if there's any more information that can be gathered from some sources that have their feet planted firmly on the ground and have not been spooked by, ahem, 'monsters.'"

I could feel my temper starting to boil up inside me. I know that my dad has, or rather had, that same capacity for a quick temper when he was young. He has used that as a sermon illustration many times.

I also knew that it would be wrong for me to give into it because he has drilled that into my head an equal number of times.

I choked back the anger and spoke as calmly as I could.

"Sis, maybe it would be better for us to go back to the spooky place with the spooky pentagram and the spooky screaming whoever or whatever, don't you think?"

"Actually, Kyle, I would suggest that you go with Carrie's suggestion on this one."

A bit bewildered, I blurted out, "Do you actually agree with her that everyone is overreacting, and there's nothing out there, because if that is the case, why are we even here? Why are we not safe and warm in our beds in our own day?"

He answered without a trace of anger at my somewhat caustic outburst.

"I am not agreeing with anyone, Kyle. I am not here for the purposes of agreement or disagreement. I am, though, here to give you some gentle nudges when I think that may be helpful. Even when," he said as he looked over at Carrie, "those nudges may or may not confirm your very strong opinions."

Carrie remained utterly poker-faced at this comment.

After an awkward few seconds of silence, he said, "I suggest you three pray and get to it. And I would also suggest you remain in an attitude of prayer as you go about your task."

Now, why would he say that I wondered? Truthfully, it sounded sort of ominous.

Nonetheless, we Warner kids never had to be asked twice to pray. We had been taught since childhood what a precious privilege it was to be able to do so, and what great power there was that came from it.

And so once again, we knelt and prayed. I knew that we would probably get up with some divisions of opinion amongst us. But for the moment all of those divisions melted away as we three banded together in prayer like a threefold cord that cannot be quickly broken.

Chapter Fifteen

The miles quickly melted away as we pedaled our way into Point Pleasant. By now we knew the way very well and had no trouble whatsoever making our way from street to street and over to the police station.

I did not know what we would find there, but by now I knew the Conductor well enough to know that he did nothing haphazardly or randomly.

Tiny's Drive-In whizzed by, and very shortly were cruising into the shadows by the police station.

We knew immediately that it would be a beneficial stop. The same two couples from two nights earlier were already there once again.

"Officer, please," I heard the first lady plead, "please believe me. We are not crazy, we are not drunk; we are in trouble. That thing has been following us for the past two nights, and now this…"

It took me a while to wrap my mind around what I was seeing. There was some kind of a lump wrapped in a blanket, and as the lady unwrapped it, I realized that I was looking at a mid-sized dog. The lady was crying now, crying hard.

The dog was not moving.

Her husband spoke, and we three Night Heroes were listening without hardly breathing.

"Buck is the best watchdog we ever had. He never barked without a reason, never disturbed the neighbors. If he ever did bark, we knew for a fact someone or something was out there. That thing followed us last night, but we were pretty sure we lost it by the time we got home. I have never driven like that in my life.

"Ten minutes after locking ourselves in the house, Buck went crazy. I was heading into the back room to get the shotgun, and then he just yelped the most horrifying sound and then stopped. No more barking from him, no more noise at all. I went out into the front yard, and this is how I found him."

The officer was kneeling over the dog by now, and I heard him say, "Someone stabbed your dog. Who in the world would do this; do you have any enemies?"

The man shook his head as if to say, "You're not really getting this," and answered, "Sir, I don't mean to try and play police officer and do your job for you, but this dog was not stabbed. Those are slashes, about finger length apart. This was done by one blow; if it had been one at a time, the dog would have run."

"What are you saying, Mister?" The officer asked as he stood. He was clearly agitated by what he suspected was being inferred.

The man did not even hesitate. "That thing killed him. I don't know what it wants or what it is trying to accomplish, but if it will do this to a dog, it will do it to a person as well."

Boy, oh boy, did that last statement ever not go over well! The officer started shouting at the man, the other man and the two ladies started shouting back, other officers started coming out of the station, it was like insanity had set in and was whipping everyone into a frenzy.

We knew it was time for us to go. Without a word, we back farther into the shadows and then started pedaling quietly away.

A mile or so outside of town we stopped to regroup.

"Well, what do you think?" I asked Carrie and Aly.

"The Moth Man," Aly answered without a moment's hesitation.

But at the exact same moment, Carrie said, "Some jerk killed a dog and is messing with everybody's mind."

The girls just glared at each other silently for a moment. I did not like where this was heading.

"Okay, skip that for a second. Let's lay aside the conjecture and go with what we know. We know for a fact that someone or something is terrorizing people around here and has now graduated to killing animals. We know that there was a scream from the TNT area. We know that at some point there have been Satan worshipers up there. It seems to me that even if we do not know or agree about what is going on, we do at least know where Ground Zero is."

"Back to the TNT area?" Carrie asked.

"I think so, Sis, yes. Unless you have any better ideas."

Carrie shook her head slowly, and Aly still looked perturbed at her sister but determined to chase down and whack a monster.

And so we pedaled.

As we did so, I tried to evaluate my own thoughts on the matter at hand. I had learned a very valuable and painful lesson in our last adventure; prejudice is a dangerous thing. If a person does not carefully and thoroughly evaluate a situation without prejudging it, he can get into some trouble.

I did not want to make that mistake here. I was heavily leaning toward the crazy idea that some, for lack of a better word, monster was actually out there. But I was still willing at this point to concede that Carrie's much more "normal" position could also be true.

As we pulled off of the road and onto the gravel and dirt of the TNT area, we coasted to a stop and sat quietly for just a moment. When I spoke, it was in a whisper.

"Well, here we are. There are thirty or forty pathways we can choose off of this main road, and a hundred or so concrete igloos to investigate, and also about eight thousand acres of woods and ponds and swamps. Where do we begin?"

"I would suggest," Carrie said in her most professorial tone, "that we begin at the exact igloo we were in earlier in the day with mom and dad."

In exasperation, Aly snapped "And how exactly do we do that? This is 1966. It's not like we can GPS it."

"We don't have to," Carrie said flatly. Then she looked over at me, held up a piece of paper with a hand-drawn map of the area and said, "Doodling."

Wow, did I feel both stupid and slightly amazed right then. Count on my genius sister to have been putting her big brain to work while the rest of us were staring out the windows like tourists.

The map she had drawn was really good. And an X marked the spot where we had been nearly fifty years from now, a little bit earlier today. The terrain would have changed, the trees and undergrowth would be different, but pathways and igloos would not have moved even a bit.

Without a word, Carrie got back on her bike and began to lead the way. It was a very well moonlit night this time, and that made me feel a lot better about all of this. But then, as I considered it, I began to wonder if that was a good thing after all. It allowed us to see where we were going better, but it also allowed whatever or whoever was out there a much better chance to see us coming.

It took about four minutes to get to the pathway we were looking for. I knew that the igloo in question was the very last one at the end of the path, seven hundred yards or so away.

We hid our bikes in some thick undergrowth and began to creep down the path very slowly and very quietly. The memory of that bloodcurdling scream from last night was still echoing in my brain. That combined with what dad had found earlier today gave me a really horrible feeling.

The moonlight trickled through the branches overhead causing wild and distorted shadows. It was almost like we were making our own monsters with every step we took.

During the daylight when we have nothing to fear there is not a single one of us who could not have done that seven hundred yards in under three minutes flat. But creeping along ultra-cautiously as we were, it took us more than a half hour to make it to the end of the pathway.

Without even having to discuss it, we had all been staying on the left side of the path, across from where we knew the igloo would be.

We stood there in the darkest of the shadows looking at the metal door yawning silently open, waiting for us.

There was no whispering. We would not dare to have risked it at that moment.

One agonizingly slow step at a time we crossed the fifteen-foot width of the pathway and got to the metal door. We stood there breathing shallowly and straining to hear any sound that was available.

There was nothing, absolutely nothing. No wind, no frogs, no crickets, no people, no monsters certainly, no nothing.

I tentatively placed a foot on the concrete pad and began to creep inside. Carrie and Aly were right behind me being just as quiet. I clicked on the LED light, scanned the entire inside of the igloo... There was nothing and no one. Step-by-step we made our way to the very center, and I shined my light down onto the ground.

Every one of us stifled back a gasp. It was there. The pentagram was there, and the lines were sharp and new and unworn. It looked like it had been made just hours ago. The stain was there too, and I knew that if I touched it, it was going to be sticky; it was still that fresh.

Horrified does not begin to describe the feeling that was running through my heart. My head was pounding, my hands were shaking...

And then everything got worse. Much worse.

Chapter Sixteen

"You dare disturb our Master's worship?"

The hissing voice came from the opening of the igloo, and we three Night Heroes instantly gasped and jumped into a defensive position to face the voice.

He was not alone. As we stood shoulder to shoulder in the center of the room, one by one figures shrouded in black robes began to enter and circle the room, completely surrounding us.

This was bad. Very bad. The three of us were now in a triangle position, making sure that we had eyes on everyone around us.

Thirteen came in. Then a pause, then another thirteen. Then a pause, then another thirteen. Thirty-nine people surrounding three.

The original speaker stepped forward and began to whisper in a low, threatening voice, almost serpent-like in its tone.

"I can smell the Jesus on you... It is a stench in my nostrils. You are no longer in church, Christians, you are now on dark and holy ground. You will now know what it means to experience real power... You will now know what it means to worship the dark lord."

Thirty-nine to three? Out of the question. There was no way to fight our way out of this one.

You know, from time to time kids say stupid things like, "What good will all of this school stuff do for me? I will never use this stuff in real life!"

Even we three Night Heroes had been guilty of saying things like that to our parents from time to time. I am glad they are good parents and did not listen to us and continued to make us apply ourselves to our studies. When Carrie spoke, it was three simple words, and it was not in English:

"Cubre tus orejas."

The devil worshiper said, "What?"

Aly and I did not say anything. We knew enough Spanish to do as Carrie had said. We immediately covered our ears tightly, and oh my goodness, even that was almost not enough. Carrie had very subtly reached in her pack for her miniature air horn. She scrunched one ear into her shoulder, covered the other with her hand, and when she cut loose with that one hundred twenty decibel sound in that echo chamber, thirty-nine black robed Satan worshipers screamed in agony with their eardrums horribly busted.

All of them were instantly on the ground writhing and crying. Just as instantly, we three Night Heroes had bolted out the door and were making world record time back down the pathway to our bikes.

We probably could have slowed down a little bit somewhere between the TNT area and the Silver Bridge. Probably, but none of us were willing to take that chance. I don't think we could have gotten there any quicker by rocket ship.

Once we got under the bridge, we laid our bikes down, and then laid ourselves down on our backs gasping for air, desperately trying to calm ourselves down.

And somewhere in the midst of that effort, we all fell asleep.

Chapter Seventeen

Thursday morning. I do not think I had ever been so thrilled to see the sun come streaming through a window. I stretched and yawned laying there on my pallet, then looked over at where my sisters would be. They were still sound asleep on their bed.

I was sort of glad of that. After all the action last night, I knew they could use the extra rest.

"GOOOOOODDDDDDD MORNING, WEST VIRGINIA!!!!"

Thanks, dad, so much for the extra rest.

I heard the girls groan, and Carrie put her pillow over her head.

But, as regular as clockwork, half an hour later we were all up and dressed and out the door. Dad took us straight to Tudor's Biscuit World again. When he has found something he likes, he will wear it out.

I was not complaining. I liked it just as much as him.

Once breakfast was done, we went back to the hotel, and then broke up and went separate ways. Mom and the girls were picked up by Mrs. Burgess and Mrs. Pinson and went to Charleston to do some shopping. Dad and I met Pastor Burgess and Pastor Pinson at the local gym and put in a couple of good hours of pushing steel.

I was glad for those couple of hours, mostly because of how much sense they made. There is weight, you push it, it goes up, you put it back down. Why could everything not be that simple? Why did there have to be things like fruitcake devil worshipers and macabre rituals and Moth Men?

But even as I asked myself the question, I already knew the answer. When mankind sinned in the garden, he opened a Pandora's box of evil that has flooded our world. Sin is always like that; it starts very small and then quickly mushrooms out of control.

Once we finished working out, we came back to the hotel and cleaned up. Then we went over to Bob Evans for some lunch, and then came back to the hotel so that dad could spend some time studying. I did the same thing. When you are a homeschooled evangelist's kid, you carry your school with you everywhere you go.

For some reason, I seemed to have an extra appreciation for my Spanish lessons on that day.

Late in the afternoon mom and the girls got back. They put aside their shopping, and we put aside our schoolwork, and everyone started getting ready for supper and for service.

Supper on this particular night was in the Fellowship Hall at the Grace Baptist Church. Some of their folks had made a delicious meal of pork chops and chicken and salad and biscuits and dessert. One thing about Baptists, they are really good with food.

We sat around talking for a while after the meal and then moseyed over into the church to get ready for service. We had a good prayer time with the men in one of the side rooms, and then service started at 7 o'clock sharp.

A church from down in Ripley had brought their choir over with them to sing. They were really good, and they sure helped to fill the place up, which I always like.

Finally, it was time for the preaching.

A lot of times I have a really good idea what my dad is going to preach. I have heard most of his messages dozens of times since he preaches some of the same messages in lots of different places. But this night was very different.

"Open your Bibles to Ephesians 6:10-16," I heard my dad say, "I want to read this text, and then preach a brand-new message that I have titled 'Do You Know What You Are Dealing With?'"

And then he began to read:

"Finally, my brethren, be strong in the Lord, and in the power of his might. Put on the whole armour of God, that ye may be able to stand against the wiles of the devil. For we wrestle not against flesh and blood, but against principalities, against powers, against the rulers of the darkness of this world, against spiritual wickedness in high places. Wherefore take unto you the whole armour of God, that ye may be able to withstand in the evil day, and having done all, to stand. Stand therefore, having your loins girt about with truth, and having on the breastplate of righteousness; And your feet shod with the preparation of the gospel of peace; Above all, taking the shield of faith, wherewith ye shall be able to quench all the fiery darts of the wicked."

The message was really good. I think all of his messages are. But this one seemed to really hit home with me because of all that we were facing and all of the unknowns concerning it. There is a very real devil who has some very real power. But we have a God who can enable us to stand against that wicked snake and come out victorious.

At least that is what I took away from the message.

There was a good response around the altar again, and I hoped that everyone was really doing business with God and getting the help that they needed.

We went back to the Bob Evans for some late-night fellowship with both of the pastors and their families and a few folks from their churches. There is not much of a better way to end the day than with laughter and pie, and we had plenty of both.

Finally, we all said our goodbyes for the night, and the Warner family made its way back to the hotel and to our room. It was time to wind down for the night; or in the case of the Night Heroes, time to get wound up.

Chapter Eighteen

"Hey, hey you two, come on, wake up, quick!"

I sat straight up on my pallet, and Aly sat straight up in bed. We were both gasping for breath again, and Carrie was kneeling between us.

I looked over at Aly and mouthed the question, "Red eyes?"

She just nodded as she tried to control her breathing.

Without another word, we all strapped on our night packs and silently slipped out of the room. Down the creepy hallway once again, through the eerie looking lobby, and out into the parking lot.

Sure enough, the Conductor was waiting for us.

"Good evening, Night Heroes, are you ready for night number four of your latest mission?"

"I believe so, Sir."

"Good. Do you intend to walk into any more traps tonight?"

"We didn't exactly intend to walk into one last night," I said somewhat sheepishly. "But I can assure you, we are going to be far more careful tonight. Especially now that we know there are a few dozen devil worshipers out there with busted eardrums and a serious grudge against us.

"If you don't mind me asking," I said thoughtfully, "what exactly is all of this about? We are starting on night four, we know that there are some people terrified out of their wits, we know there are some others doing their little devil worship thing under the cover of darkness, but we have no idea what the end game is. That makes it a little bit hard for us to know what we need to do to win, or even to know how we will know if we have won. What exactly are they trying to accomplish, and what exactly are we supposed to be trying to accomplish?"

He stood there for a moment as if considering what he could or should say. Then, just as Jesus often did, he answered a question with a question.

"What do you think this is all about, what do each of you think this is about? You first, Kyle."

"Well," I said measuring my words, "I, I honestly just don't know. Is that an acceptable answer?"

"It is an honest answer," he said, "and therefore it is most certainly acceptable. Carrie, what about you?"

She did not even hesitate. "I think there are flesh and blood people trying to spook everyone. I think they are doing the entire black robe/devil worship routine to cover up some illegal activity they are involved in. I believe they are trying to keep everyone scared away from the TNT area so they can do their drugs or sell their stolen goods or whatever illegal and immoral things they are trying to hide. I believe this Moth Man thing is their way of spreading the word that no one needs to be around their private little playground. I don't know how they are making people see things, but I intend to find out."

He nodded, neither in agreement or disagreement, merely in a sign that he heard her and understood what she was saying. Then he turned to Aly.

"What about you, Aly?"

"I love my sister, Sir, but I could not disagree with her more on this one. Everything she says would make sense except for the fact that on the first night here all three of us woke

131

up with that dream of red eyes. I believe there is far more to it than just human mischief-making. I really don't know what, but there is something out there."

He nodded once again and then said, "One has a strong opinion on one end of the spectrum, another has a strong opinion on the other end of the spectrum, and the other does not yet know what to think. Can the three of you manage to pull together and see this through despite your differing positions?"

"Yes sir," we all answered immediately. Then I spoke up for all of us.

"We may not be in agreement on what we are facing, but I know some things we do agree on. We love the Lord, we love each other, and we know that He has brought us here for a reason. We don't have to be in agreement to be on the same side. The disciples often argued among themselves, but at the end of the day there were unified in following Jesus."

"Good, Kyle, good. I can assure you that you will need that very unity in this mission and in every other one you face." Then he turned to the girls and said much more ominously, "However, only one of the two of you can be right. And that will make all the difference in the world as to how you deal with what you are facing."

We did not have to be told what to do next. We knelt and poured our hearts out to

God one more time. If there is anywhere that divisions melt away, it is before the throne of God who has redeemed us all.

When we were done praying, we rose from our knees, and the Conductor was gone. Without a word, we mounted our metallic steeds one more time and began to pedal. Thirty-five minutes of pedaling and praying and pondering and planning, I just hoped that would be enough by the time we arrived.

As we pulled onto the gravel and dirt of the TNT area one more time, we braked to a stop and faced each other to lay our plans for the night.

"Well, night four guys. We get this thing solved tonight or tomorrow night, or we don't get it solved at all. This is our seventh mission, and our first six have all taken all five nights. What do you think? Can we take names and kick fannies and get this done tonight?"

"Yes," Carrie said confidently. "We made a great start last night. I guarantee you there are thirty-nine people lying in bed with ice on their heads who will not be causing us any problems tonight. I say we go in, figuratively speaking, with guns blazing, smoke out the rest of the cockroaches, and put the 'Moth Man' to rest."

"Sis," I said kindly as I put my hands on her shoulders and looked her eyeball to eyeball, "do you remember in 1 Kings chapter 20 when the king of Syria threatened the king of Israel? The king of Israel sent him back a message basically saying, 'Don't brag like someone who has just won the battle and is taking off their armor when you haven't even put your armor on yet to fight the battle.' You might want to dial back that overconfidence just a bit; it will do nothing but cause you trouble. And if it causes YOU trouble, it will cause US trouble."

"I understand, Kyle, and I will be careful. I just don't think these yahoos are nearly as big of a deal as the threats we have dealt with in the past. I mean," she said as she considered those words, "the much more distant past..."

I let the matter drop, and we begin to smoothly cycle toward our destination, the very spot we parked last night. We really did not know what else to do; we just determined to pick up where we left off last night.

We arrived at the right pathway, parked our bikes, took our hike as quietly as ghosts, and soon arrived across from last night's echoing igloo.

"Okay, I whispered, I have a two-part proposal to make. First, I propose that we do not get trapped in the spooky concrete tomb again. Are we all agreed?"

"Agreed," Carrie and Aly whispered back.

"Okay then; part two. I propose that we turn the tables on our enemy or enemies. Last night they trapped us. Let's return the favor."

Aly smiled a devious looking smile. "That, Big Brother, sounds like more fun than a snow-covered Christmas morning. Let's do it. What's your plan?"

The plan was simple, really, at least as far as I was concerned. I opened my night pack and pulled out two containers of pepper spray. Dad, Mr. Security, keeps a couple of them in every vehicle just in case any of the Warner ladies ever need to blast anybody. I took them out of the Yukon last night and carried them to bed with me.

"These, Lady Night Heroes, will put down a large pack of man or beast. Now, all we need is to get into position and to bait the hook."

"Bait the hook, Kyle?" Carrie asked with a not very reassured look. "Exactly what do you intend to use for bait, and where do you intend to throw the hook?"

"I intend to throw the hook in the most sensible of all places, Sis, right where the fish have been biting." As I said that I that pointed toward the igloo and the steel doors that were gaping open menacingly. "And as for bait, I

135

cannot think of a better worm than one of us. Two of us will be to the side and on top of the igloo, hidden in the brush, ready to unleash the pepper spray. The other one will be inside the igloo making worm noises..."

"Worm noises? Seriously?"

"Hey, Sis, if you can spout off Spanish on the spur of the moment in an emergency situation, surely you can come up with some convincing worm noises."

Carrie shook her head in apparent irritation and simply said, "Fine. Worm noises it is. Anything to expose these punks and bring their game to an end."

"Excellent. Give Aly and I time to work our way into position. I will whistle a Nut Hatcher call when I am set Aly, you whistle a Goldfinch call when you are set."

I began to creep to the left and Aly begin to creep to the right. We went slowly; oh, so very slow. For the trap to be set right, no one could know that we were there.

It is a funny thing at times like that, the crazy things that go through your mind. I wanted to get into position without making a sound, but I also wanted to beat Aly to the whistle. It just wouldn't be good if my little sister was quicker than me. I guess that is that old pride that all of us have to contend with.

Twenty minutes later I was within six feet of my goal.

"Peesa Peesa Peesa Peesa Peesa Peesa Peesa Peesa Peesa!"

Rats. She beat me by thirty seconds. Grrrrrrrr. I covered the remaining few feet and gave my signal.

"Wheep Wheep Wheep Wheep Wheep Wheep Wheep Wheep!"

Carrie calmly got up from her place, click on the flashlight, and walked across the pathway into the igloo without so much as slowing down. A few quiet seconds passed, and I began to get very nervous.

"So," I heard her voice echo, "no one is home tonight. Well, don't mind me while I have a little worship service then..."

I could not believe what I heard next. If she was wanting to get attention from devil worshipers, she was definitely going to accomplish it. She was standing in the igloo, no doubt right on top of that stupid pentagram, singing what has often been called the Christian national anthem:

"Amazing grace how sweet the sound that saved a wretch like me, I once was lost, but now I'm found was blind, but now I see...

One verse down, and Carrie was just getting warmed up:

"Thru many dangers toils and snares, I have already come, 'tis grace that brought me safe thus far, and grace will lead..."

Will lead? That isn't how the verse ends, Sis. Sing "Me home..." Come on, Carrie, give me the "me home."

A few seconds passed, and those two expected words did not come. I could feel the hot fear rising up in my throat. Something was wrong. I clicked my flashlight over toward where Aly should be and caught sight of her face. Her eyes were wide, and panic was written all over her. She knew that something was wrong too.

Caution? Nope, time to throw that to the wind.

"Stay," I shouted at Aly. And I reached over and grabbed the edge of the igloo and swung in at an angle, feet first. I landed on my knees, with one arm up in a defensive position, but I quickly realized that there was no defense for what we had walked into.

Chapter Nineteen

I knew that when Carrie had walked into the igloo, it was completely empty. Otherwise, she would not have needed to go the "Amazing Grace" route to draw attention. I also knew that there was only one way in and one way out and that no one had come in after her.

But there was one more thing I knew at that moment; I knew that there were three of us in that room.

There is probably no way I can accurately describe the terror that I was feeling at that moment, but I will try. Carrie was standing in the middle of the room, looking like her feet were rooted to the ground, but shaking like a leaf on a tree. Her eyes were wide and terrified. Standing over her, at least seven-feet tall, was the most evil looking creature I had ever seen. He was vaguely shaped like a man but had taloned feet, long, razor-sharp claws on his hands, black wings that looked like they were made of smoke from the pit of hell itself, and the most devilish looking red eyes you could ever imagine.

He was standing over my sister. He was standing over my sister!

The next thing I knew, I was doing the only thing that I knew how to do, rushing toward him ready to fight and die for my sister.

That did not last long, nor did it go well. This creature moved faster than any human being I have ever fought. Like lightning, he pulled his clawed fist back and backhanded me across the side of the head. The last thing I remember was shouting for Carrie to run while I hit the ground, and everything went completely black...

Hey, everyone, this is Carrie, I will pick the story up from here.

When I walked into the center of that room and started singing Amazing Grace, I must confess that I was not being nearly as spiritual as the song sounded. Truthfully, I was irritated and perturbed and absolutely in the flesh. I was quite certain that we were dealing with human mischief makers, and human mischief makers really annoy me.

My entire opinion changed the instant that creature walked through the solid concrete wall and stood over me. I could not move or speak, but he had some things to say.

"So," he hissed in an ominous whisper, "this is one of the great Night Heroes? I am, shall we say, less than impressed. This is the girl that the so-called God has blessed with such intelligence? And yet here you are standing in my domain defenseless and about to die. Be sure and give your God my most unkind regards after I have slashed you to pieces and sent you to meet Him."

That was the exact moment that Kyle came flying into the room. A split second later he was rushing this thing, and just as quickly, it had smashed him across the head and sent him flying into the wall. I remember him screaming for me to run. He would not have had to tell me that; I knew that I had to run just to get him to follow me and leave my now defenseless brother alone. Kyle risked his life for me, and I was not going to leave this thing in the room with him.

"Catch me if you can, you fat overgrown housefly!" I screamed at him as I ran from the igloo. I wanted to make sure he was furious enough to follow me.

He was.

I bolted out of that concrete room faster than I have ever moved in my life. I could hear wings hungrily gulping the air behind me. I burst across the pathway and into the thick woods on the other side. There was no more thought of subtlety whatsoever. I was crashing through branches, stumbling over logs, and loudly sloshing through creeks and bogs. I knew in my mind that Kyle was still back there in the igloo, but I had no ability for rational thought at that moment. I was screaming and looking for him, and screaming and looking for Aly, even though they were both far behind.

But the noise behind me was greater still. Trees were crashing and splintering, and there was a demonic roaring echoing through the woods.

I was giving it everything I had, absolutely everything, but it did not take me long to realize that it was no use. Even with my small head start and the ability to go between trees, this thing was going through the trees, and the noise behind me was getting closer and closer. I knew that soon he would catch me.

My breath was coming in gasps, and I could feel the tears stinging my eyes as I ran, panicked, through the pitch-black West Virginia night. There was no use telling me that there is no such thing as the Moth Man. Yesterday, I would have agreed with you, but now I could not shake him, nor could I find Kyle or Aly, and I knew I was going to die...

And then, just like every grade B horror movie ever made, I tripped. Why, oh why, does the girl always have to trip?

My face dug into the moss, and I quickly rolled over and spat it out as I backed up against a log. I wanted to back up much, much farther, really, I did, since I was staring right at this vision of evil that had changed my mind in an instant about monsters, but there was nowhere else for me to go.

"Congratulations," he said with an evil laugh, "you have caused me quite a bit of exertion tonight. Fortunately, since I am an eternal being, I will be just fine. You on the other hand…"

"Wait," I said with my mind racing, trying to buy an extra second or two, "it is abundantly clear that I have lost. I can't get away from you; I can't beat you. So, since you have nothing to lose, may I at least ask you a question before you kill me?"

The creature seemed amused by that and bowed dramatically.

"The genius Christian girl seeks after my dark wisdom? Why, of course, child, what is it you wish to know before I send you to meet your Maker?"

"I wish to know what the point of all this is. What is your purpose with this town and these people?"

"Do you not know?" He asked sarcastically. "You 'great heroes,' " he said those last two words even more sarcastically, "were sent here to stop me from establishing an open point of worship for my dark lord. For thousands of years now since he was unjustly cast out of heaven, he has been worshiped only in the darkness and in the shadows.

"But the time has come for all of that to change. People are abandoning your God in droves. Drugs and the free love revolution are all the rage now. My lord has raised a generation that will worship him since he is the one that will give them all of the desires of their flesh, while your God requires that people deny the desires of their flesh.

"Every great thing must start small, but every great thing must start. This tiny town will be the birthplace of something much greater. I will instill such fear and awe into everyone that they will turn anywhere that will promise them refuge.

"Once the entire area is terrified to death of me, my dark lord's servants will be the evangelists that tell everyone that if they will worship him, he will protect them from the demon that has been terrorizing them."

I started to speak, trying to buy just a little more time, but that did not work out so well.

"Be silent before me, girl," he shrieked. "You have received your answer but in vain. As one of your prophets said, 'prepare to meet thy God.'"

The monster stood directly over me and raised a clawed hand. This was it; I really was going to die.

"She won't be meeting Him tonight," a voice from behind him very calmly said. It was Aly!

"You!" the demon howled as he whirled around. "What do you have to say about it? I shall kill her and then I shall kill you and then I shall go and very slowly kill your brother!"

He was spitting mad as he got to that last word. But Aly, I could not understand it, Aly looked as calm as if she was sitting on dad's lap with his arms wrapped around her.

"No, actually, you won't kill her, and you won't kill me, and you won't kill my brother. You also won't terrorize this area anymore, and your dark lord will not use this town to begin his open worship in our society."

Oh, my goodness, rage does not begin to describe it! That thing screamed like a million banshees, and while I lay there paralyzed in fear, rushed at my little sister.

She made exactly one movement. She raised her hand in front of her in the universal symbol for "stop."

And it did. As if it had hit a brick wall, it stopped right in front of her. Its clawed hand was raised and ready to kill.

And then Aly did the most unthinkable thing: she took a step toward it.

It took a step backward.

Then it began to fumble about for words, "I, I don't understand, what…"

"Let me spell it out for you. 1 John 4:4, 'Ye are of God, little children, and have overcome them: because greater is he that is in you, than he that is in the world.'"

She took another step forward, the thing took another step backward, and it clasped its hands over its ears in horror.

"Don't like that one? How about this one? Revelation 12:11, 'And they overcame him by the blood of the Lamb, and by the word of their testimony; and they loved not their lives unto the death.'"

"How! How are you..."

"My dad preached about it last night. Ephesians 6:12-16, 'For we wrestle not against flesh and blood, but against principalities, against powers, against the rulers of the darkness of this world, against spiritual wickedness in high places. Wherefore take unto you the whole armour of God, that ye may be able to withstand in the evil day, and having done all, to stand. Stand therefore, having your loins girt about with truth, and having on the breastplate of righteousness;

And your feet shod with the preparation of the gospel of peace; Above all, taking the shield of faith, wherewith ye shall be able to quench all the fiery darts of the wicked.'

"I know what you are. You are a fallen angel, a demon. But I also know what I am; I am a blood bought, born-again, Holy Spirit-filled child of the living God."

When she said that, the creature doubled over as if someone had kicked it in the gut. But Aly was not done, not by a long shot.

"Your dark lord has already been defeated. When my Jesus died on Calvary and then rose from the dead, Satan's power was crushed. He is already ruined; he just doesn't know it. And just like my Jesus, 2000 years ago, cast thousands of demons out of a man and sent them out of the area, in His name and by His power I am telling you to leave and never come back."

"I... I will be feared and worshiped!" It sputtered.

"You will be a tinfoil tourist attraction on Main Street," Aly countered, "no more believable than Sasquatch or the Loch Ness monster."

She took one more step toward him and then deliver the deathblow:

"In the name of Jesus Christ of Nazareth, the son of the living God, my Lord and Savior, the King of kings and Lord of lords, I am commanding you to immediately leave this area and never return."

With a shriek of anguish and defeat the creature whirled and took flight, and as it and the sound of its ruin faded into the dark West Virginia night, I knew that it would never be back.

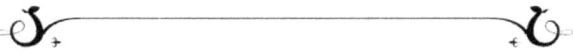

Aly and I found Kyle knocked out cold right where he had landed in the igloo. It took a few minutes of shaking him and calling his name, but finally, his eyes popped open.

"Whu, wha happened?"

"We have a lot of catching up to do, my dear brother. Let's just put it this way. I am glad that thing back-handed you instead of ripping you to shreds with his claws. Thanks for being willing to lay down your life for mine; I appreciate that. As for our littlest sister here, tonight she turned out to be the biggest Night Hero of all.

Kyle just looked at her groggily and smiled and held out his fist for a fist bump.

"Nice job, Squirt."

"Thanks, Big Brother. Do you think you can ride?"

"Oh yeah," he said with a strengthening smile, "I can ride."

And so we did. Back into the night, and back to our own time. Tomorrow I would ask dad if we could go into downtown Point Pleasant one more time.

There was a statue I wanted to stick my tongue out at.

Coming Soon:

Runaway

"You sho you three young uns know what you gittin yoselves into? Master Feeney, he's a sho-nuf devil when he git crossed. Got a bad temper... as like to kill a man as speak to him. And don't think he gonna show you no mercy cause you kids: he'll cut yo throat as fast as he would three full grown men."

I just smiled at this dear old man, then calmly replied, "Joe, don't you worry about us. You just be ready to go come midnight. You are going to see your sweet Mabel again; and with God's power on our side, I pity Mr. Feeney or anyone else who tries to stand in our way."

Other Books in the Night Heroes Series

Other Books by Dr. Wagner

From Footers to Finish Nails

Beyond the Colored Coat

Daniel: Breathtaking

Esther: Five Feasts and the Fingerprints of God

Nehemiah: A Labor of Love

Marriage Makers/Marriage Breakers

I'm Saved! Now What???

Don't Muzzle the Ox

Romans: Salvation from A-Z